D.J. was within twenty feet of the cabin door before the watching dog moved. Silently, with his head down, the dog ran toward the boy. D.J. turned and dashed madly toward the cabin.

He shifted the lamp to his left hand with the matches and desperately twisted the doorknob. As the door opened, D.J. leaped inside and slammed the door shut with his heel. He set the lamp and matches down on the floor and used both hands to jerk the wood box against the door. Then D.J. collapsed against it, his heart thumping so hard he could feel the blood pounding in his ears.

LEE RODDY is a former staff writer and researcher for a movie production company. He lives in the Sierra Nevada Mountains of California and devotes his time to writing books and public speaking. He is a cowriter of the book which became the TV series, "The Life and Times of Grizzly Adams."

Born on an Illinois farm and reared on a California ranch, Lee Roddy grew up around hunters and trail hounds. As a boy, he began writing animal stories. He spent lots of time reading about dogs, horses, and other animals. These stories shaped his thinking and values before he went to Hollywood to write professionally. His Christian commitment later turned his writing talents to books like this one. This is the fifth book in the D.J. Dillon Adventure Series.

Mad Dog of Lobo Mountain

LEE RODDY

VICTOR BOOKS®
A DIVISION OF SCRIPTURE PRESS PUBLICATIONS INC.
USA CANADA ENGLAND

THE D.J. DILLON ADVENTURE SERIES

THE HAIR-PULLING BEAR DOG
THE CITY BEAR'S ADVENTURES
DOOGER, THE GRASSHOPPER HOUND
GHOST DOG OF STONEY RIDGE
MAD DOG OF LOBO MOUNTAIN
THE LEGEND OF THE WHITE RACCOON
THE MYSTERY OF THE BLACK HOLE MINE
GHOST OF THE MOANING MANSION
THE HERMIT OF MAD RIVER
ESCAPE DOWN THE RAGING RAPIDS

4 5 6 7 8 9 10 Printing/Year 94 93 92 91

All Scripture quotations are from the *King James Version*.

Library of Congress Catalog Card Number: 86-60859
ISBN: 0-89693-482-9

VICTOR BOOKS
A division of SP Publications, Inc.
Wheaton, Illinois 60187

CONTENTS

To
Lucille "Momma Lu" Roddy,
"Keturah" to my father,
the finest second mother
anyone could have

Chapter One

DANGER ON THE TRAIL

D.J. Dillon was worried. He again whistled for his
little dog, Hero, but the soaring mountains with their
dense rows of tall timber swallowed up the sound.
There was no answering joyful bark. Instead, in the
distance, a long, angry blast of a car horn echoed
through the evergreen trees and bounced off the
granite face of Devil's Point before fading away into
silence.

The boy was slender as a ski pole. He turned his
blue eyes upon his best friend, Alfred Milford, a skinny
boy with thick eyeglasses.

"Dad's getting impatient, but I can't just go off and
leave Hero in this wilderness."

"You shouldn't have taken him off his leash, D.J."

"I know! I know! But Hero usually obeys real well,
yet when he struck that trail—it must have been really
fresh—he just took off. Oh no—there's Dad's horn
again. He's really leaning on it!"

Alfred used his right thumb to push his thick-lensed glasses higher up on his nose. "Maybe if we ask him, he'll let us stay here and look for your dog while he goes on to Lake Tahoe."

Alfred was so thin D.J. could see his best friend's ribs through the old blue work shirt that had once been Mr. Milford's.

D.J. brushed his pale yellowish hair back from his eyes. He was quite tall for his thirteen years. "Come on! Let's go ask."

As the two boys came slipping and sliding down California's Sierra Nevada Mountains at the 5,000-foot level, D.J. caught a glimpse of his father through the ten-story-tall conifers.* Sam Dillon was standing outside the sedan he'd bought since marrying D.J.'s stepmother. Dad shaded his deeply tanned face against the late morning sun that filtered through the heavy shadows of the roadside campground.

Sam Dillon was a short but powerfully built man who made his living as a choke-setter* in the timber. His huge chest seemed out of proportion to his short legs. He stretched his muscular forearm into the open car window and gave the horn several long blasts.

D.J. slipped and fell on his hands and knees in the slippery brown pine needles. He landed in some mountain misery.* He jumped up quickly, sputtering at the terrible smell of the low-growing fernlike plants.

From the narrow trail behind him, Alfred asked, "You OK, D.J.?"

"Yeah, just skinned my hands a little," D.J. said,

*You can find an explanation of the starred words under "Life in Stoney Ridge" on pages 122-126.

brushing them against nearly new jeans. "Let's go on. Wait—listen!"

"You hear Hero?"

"No, listen!" D.J. held up both his hands and cocked his head. An angry voice filled the campground below.

"Hey, you with the horn! Cut it out!"

For a moment, D.J. listened fearfully, half expecting his father's hair-trigger temper to go off. Even when D.J.'s mother was alive, before she was killed in a car wreck a long time ago, Dad was full of meanness and fight. He didn't take anything off anybody, no matter how big the other person might be. But Dad had been different since Brother Paul Stagg had come to Stoney Ridge.

"Sorry, Mister," D.J. heard his father say, "I'm in a hurry and I was trying to call my son in. . . ."

The angry stranger's voice interrupted. "Well knock it off!"

Dad's reply was instant. "I *said* I was sorry!"

D.J. scrambled down the trail, not even turning his head to look at Alfred. "Come on! Faster! I don't know how much pushing Dad will take anymore!"

The two boys soon rounded a curve in the narrow hiking trail as it leveled out at the campground. D.J. sprinted in dusty tennis shoes through the Douglas fir, ponderosa pines,* and incense cedar that covered the entire campground with shadows.

D.J. raced across the gravel road that led among the various campsites. There weren't many people in the camp, but what few there were had come outside their tents or campers to look toward the sound of the angry voice.

D.J. saw his father first. Sam Dillon was standing with his legs slightly apart and braced. He was rubbing the back of his right hand inside the calloused palm of his left hand. From a distance, D.J. could see his dad's face was darkening as his temper slipped away.

D.J. saw the other man too. He was about Dad's age, but at least a foot taller. He wore black motorcycle boots, leather pants, and a dirty white T-shirt that exposed several blue tattoos on heavily muscled biceps and forearms. D.J. could see that the man had a wild black beard that hadn't been trimmed in years. A red and blue bandana kept his uncut dark hair out of his eyes.

As the stranger started around a picnic table toward Dad, D.J. yelled, "Hey, Dad! We're coming! We're coming!"

The boy saw his father turn in his direction. Then Dad said something softly to the bearded man. D.J. couldn't hear Dad's words, but the stranger stopped. His reply wasn't clear, but there was an angry sound in his voice.

D.J. called, "Come on, Alfred!" He ran off the side of Devil's Point and onto the flat campground area. D.J. raced around the few tents and pickups with campers. He ran straight to the Dillon sedan and jerked the front passenger's door open. Alfred did the same in the backseat.

"Let's go on to Lake Tahoe! Please, Dad?"

Sam Dillon took a slow deep breath and turned away from the bearded and tattooed stranger. He also turned slowly and started walking back toward a dusty old camper parked by a Douglas fir.

Dad slid under the wheel. "Where's your dog, D.J.?"

"He struck a trail and ran off. Alfred and I tried to call him back, but it must have been a bear's scent or something, because Hero. . . "

Dad interrupted. "D.J., how many times have I told you to make sure a dog obeys *every* time?"

"Ah, Dad—you know Hero's usually so good. . . "

Dad interrupted again, starting the engine with quick motions. "And did you ever get around to getting his license?"

"I told you, Dad! Hero has to have his rabies vaccination before they'll license him! And I just haven't had the time."

Dad let the clutch out so fast the car jumped and threw up dust. "You're old enough to take *full* responsibility for such things, D.J.!"

The boy started to answer, but changed his mind. He wanted to get away from the angry man in the campground before asking Dad about staying behind to look for the lost dog. Up until recently, Dad would have been fighting the stranger and somebody would have called the sheriff's office.

It had been that way for years, until not long ago when the lay preacher, Brother Paul Stagg, had helped Sam Dillon get his life changed through faith in God. Still, D.J. wasn't sure how much of a test his dad was ready to handle.

The car bounced over the rutted dirt road and slowed down beside the unattended gate. Dust kicked up behind the sedan and swirled past the car. For a moment, D.J. could barely see the signs posted by the open gate. He remembered the words from when they had entered a half hour or so before.

"Devil's Point Public Campground. Timbergold County. Honor system. Deposit $3.00 per 24-hour period. Pets must be on leash at all times. Fourteen-day camping limit."

There were some other smaller signs, including one that said, **Rabies Warning!** But D.J. hadn't stopped to read them.

He knew he had to speak fast. "Dad, we just can't go off and leave my dog!"

"You know I've got to get to Lake Tahoe to meet that man at noon, and you've already cost us twenty minutes we don't have to spare!"

"But Dad! . . ."

Sam Dillon interrupted again. "I used to leave my trail hounds lots of times! Like when I'd have to go to work and they were out of earshot for the recall horn, I'd just leave an old coat or something for them and then I'd drive away. After a day or two, when they got tired running a 'coon, they'd come back to where I'd left the coat. Your mutt's half hound, so he'll do the same."

"Ah, Dad!"

"You just have to leave something of yours, so the dog'll stay with it. Right over there by that burned-out stump's a good place. Jump out and leave your undershirt or something."

The boy started to protest again, but realized Dad was being nice, all things considered. D.J. got out of the sedan and unbuttoned his shirt. He removed it quickly and started to slip his white undershirt over his head. A picture fell out of the shirt pocket. D.J.

picked it up and glanced at Dad.

"It's the color picture Two Mom took of me and Hero a couple of weeks ago," he said, replacing the photo. Then the boy finished removing his undershirt. It was old and getting holes in it. Soon his stepmother, Two Mom, would be using it for a dust rag, anyway.

The boy quickly rubbed the undershirt over his chest to increase his body smell for the dog. Then D.J. dropped the garment on the ground and used his tennis shoes to kick the undershirt against the stump. He pulled his shirt back on and buttoned it as he slid back into the front seat beside his father.

Alfred asked from the backseat, "Will some of the campers be likely to pick that shirt up, D.J.?"

"I hope not."

"Shirt's worthless," Dad said, letting the clutch out. "Nobody'll touch it. Now, buckle up because we've got a lot of climbing to do to make that appointment on time."

* * * * *

D.J. was so concerned about leaving his little hair-pulling bear dog* behind that he didn't pay much attention to the trip toward the Nevada state line. Soon they passed the mountain's summit and dropped down toward Lake Tahoe. The huge, deep high mountain body of water stood partly in green, timbered California and partly in Nevada with its arid desert lands.

On the California side of the border, D.J. was still in Timbergold County. It stretched from the gold country foothills of the Mother Lode on the west to the timber and recreation areas of South Lake Tahoe and the Nevada border on the east.

Dad reached his appointment just twenty minutes late. D.J. and Alfred walked along the shore while Dad and the man talked in the shade of a lightning-shattered ponderosa.

D.J. tried not to worry about Hero, but the boy barely saw the deep blue water with the streaks of pale green that made it so beautiful. D.J. didn't say much to Alfred, either, but his best friend understood. Finally, Dad finished his business and they started back down the mountain highway.

"I probably wasted my time," he summarized. "I don't think he really wants to dicker.* Well, anyway, it's a good day for a drive. We could get home before supper if we don't have to waste too much time looking for your dog, D.J."

In an hour or so, they had wound down the mountain highway toward the 5,000-foot level, still a couple of hours away from Sacramento, the state capital, that stood in the valley below the Sierras. D.J.'s lips were dry when they approached the campground.

Both boys looked for Hero along the roadside as the car slowed. But they saw nothing. Dad turned off of the paved highway onto the dusty road that led back into the campground. As the sedan eased past the untended gate, D.J.'s blue eyes went instantly to the stump where he had left the shirt. It was exactly where he had put it. The boy's heart slipped down to his ankles.

"He's not back, Dad!"

"Well, guess you'll have to go look, boys. I'll drive around to the far side, as close to the mountain as I can get. You go back up where you last saw him. I'll wait by the car for half an hour. You understand? No more! Then we're heading on home!"

D.J. wanted to say something about staying away from the man with the black beard, but the boy knew that wasn't a smart thing to do. Dad had probably deliberately driven around the center of camp to avoid running into the man.

Devil's Point rose like a slab of solid granite from the evergreen trees. Near the top, centuries of storms, melting snow water, and unchecked winds had scoured off all trees and shrubs. The gray peak stood like a spear point above the timberline. A huge patch of snow still rested in the northeast crevice though it was late June and the sun was bright and hot.

"Terrible place to get lost," Alfred said as the boys got out of the car.

"Yeah," D.J. agreed. He led the way back through the deep shadows toward the start of the mountain where Hero had dashed off into the brush.

Alfred said, "Sure hope that guy with the tattoos stays away from your father."

"Me too."

As the boys rounded a large green tent in the heavy shade of late afternoon, D.J. saw the bearded man. He was cussing something fierce, D.J. heard. A 4-foot-tall boy of about 7 or 8 was crying. He wore only a pair of cutoff jeans. A barefoot woman with a shapeless sack dress and long uncombed hair was washing the kid's right hand under an outdoor water faucet.

There was no way to go around the man, woman, and boy without deliberately swinging away. D.J.

swallowed hard and walked up to them.

"Excuse me," D.J. said quietly, "is he OK?"

"Dog bit him," the woman explained, scrubbing the crying child's hands with soap.

"I'm sorry," D.J. said.

The tatooed man growled through his wild black beard. "Bite don't amount to much, but they've got rabies warning signs posted over by the gate. The dog ran away, so if we can't find him, my kid'll have to have those rabies shots. I hear they're painful as. . . . "

The little boy let out a frightened squall. "I don't want no shots!"

"Shut up!" the man snapped, drawing back his hand as though he were going to slap the kid. "You'll get them if I say so!"

"No, I won't!"

D.J. didn't want to get caught in a family squabble. "Excuse me, but we're looking for my dog. He's lost. He's about. . . . "

The tattooed man looked up suddenly. His dark eyes snapped with cold fury. "If your dog bit my kid—"

"No! No!" D.J. interrupted. "Hero wouldn't bite *anybody.*"

The child went on squalling while his father towered over D.J. and Alfred. The man asked, "What's your dog look like?"

"Well, sir," D.J. began, "he's sort of a mixture of hound, Airedale, and Australian shepherd. He's kind of reddish-brown, shaggy-like, with a stub tail. Wait—I've got a picture!"

D.J. reached into his shirt pocket and pulled out

the color photo. "You can see he's not very big, but. . . ."

D.J.'s voice trailed off as the man suddenly grabbed the picture, bent over, and thrust the photo in front of the crying kid. "Is that him, Roger?"

The little boy rubbed his nose with his left hand and tried to stop sniffling. He looked at the photograph.

"That's him! *That's* the dog that bit me!"

The man swore loudly and straightened up. He threw the picture at D.J.'s feet. "Kid, I'm going to get my gun and go after your dog! When I finish with him, I'll take care of you too!"

Chapter Two

DOUBLE TROUBLE FOR D.J.

For a moment, D.J. stood in stunned silence. Then he turned to Alfred. His hazel eyes widened through the thick glasses that some kids said looked like the bottom of a soda-pop bottle.

"What'll we do, D.J.?"

The barefoot woman turned off the water faucet and dried her small son's hands. "If I was you boys, I'd hope my husband don't find your dog!"

D.J. scoffed, "I tried to tell him—*my* dog wouldn't bite anybody, especially a little kid!"

The woman spoke over her son's cries. "My husband done shot a dog in our neighborhood last year. It got out of its yard and chased Roger."

"But Hero's innocent!" D.J. protested, raising both hands in an excited gesture.

"You won't never prove that to him," the woman said, nodding toward a dusty camper on a pickup truck. "See?"

D.J. saw. The tattooed man came out of the single narrow door at the rear of the camper. He had put a wide-brimmed leather hat on his wild hair. He stopped in the brown pine needles to strap a big holstered pistol around his waist.

The woman lowered her voice to a whisper. "That's a .357 Magnum revolver! He says it'll blow a hole in a car engine big enough to drive a tractor through."

Being a mountain boy, D.J. knew something about guns. He didn't doubt what the terrible weapon would do to Hero if the man found the dog.

"I'm sorry about your little boy," D.J. said, forcing his eyes away from the tattooed man. D.J. knelt and took the boy's hand. "OK if I look?"

The boy stopped crying and held out his hand. D.J. saw that the wound seemed clean. Yet he knew from his part-time work as a stringer* for the *Timbergold Gazette* that it didn't even take a bite to transmit the rabies virus. It lived in the saliva of an infected animal, and getting the saliva on an open cut could also cause the terrible disease.

D.J. also remembered that when someone was bitten and the animal wasn't found, doctors usually gave the antirabies injections to make sure the person was protected from the hydrophobia* virus. Otherwise, the victim would die.

"I'm sorry you got hurt—Roger—is that your name?"

The little boy nodded and D.J. continued. "I'm sorry you got bitten, but I know my dog didn't do it."

"The dog looked like the picture," Roger said, sniffing loudly.

"You wouldn't want my dog hurt because some other dog bit you, would you, Roger?" D.J. continued.

The boy shook his head. His mother dried her hands on a yellow towel and gently shoved the boy toward the camper.

"Roger, you go with your father. He'll want to know where you were when it happened. Then you come straight back and we'll go see the doctor."

"No! No! I don't *want* no doctor! I don't *want* no shots!" the child yelled, starting to cry.

His father's angry voice prevented a reply. "Come here, Boy! Show me where that dog was when you got bit!"

"I don't want no shots!"

"Come here, I said!"

Reluctantly, Roger obeyed. The tattooed man took his son's small unhurt hand and started up the trail the way the boy pointed. It was the same area where Hero had run off.

The mother raised her voice. "Will you bring him back, Bake?"

The man swung his head around sharply and angrily replied. "It's only right over there by the edge of the campground, Nelda! He's big enough to come back by himself!"

The mother looked unsure, but D.J. figured she wasn't likely to argue with her husband. The man and little boy became indistinct shadows in the deeper shadows of the big trees.

Slowly, the woman turned from watching her husband and son where they had disappeared. She looked down on D.J.

"I've got to take Roger into town and see what the

doctor says. But I know they'll want to give him those shots—just to be safe."

D.J. frowned, trying to remember something. "The editor of the weekly newspaper at Indian Springs ran a story about two rabid dogs last December or January. I think it said doctors will wait a few days before starting the shots in case somebody finds the dog. If the dog's had a rabies vaccination, then I don't think the bitten person has to take the shots."

"Your dog had his rabies shot?" The woman's question was blunt.

D.J. swallowed hard. "No, not yet. You see, I was going to have them done so I could get Hero's license. . . ."

The woman interrupted. "Then how do *you* know your dog couldn't have rabies?"

"Oh, I keep him clean and everything! He's very healthy!"

"Does he ever run loose?"

"Well, sure. He's a hair-pulling bear dog, so sometimes he runs in the woods, like now. . . . " D.J. stopped, realizing what he was saying.

"Then he could have been bitten by a rabid animal, and your dog could also be going mad with hydrophobia and you might not know it!"

"Missus, Hero was as healthy this morning as the day he was born!"

"But if he had been infected, maybe the symptoms didn't show until when he bit Roger!"

"Hero wouldn't bite!"

The woman replied, "There's only one way to prove that. Find your dog before my husband does."

Alfred had been silent, but suddenly he blurted out, "She's right, D.J.!"

"They'd keep your dog penned up for a few days until they're sure," the woman said.

D.J.'s eyes lit up, then he frowned. "No, that won't do, entirely, either. Some dog did bite your boy, and it wasn't Hero—so that other dog's got to be found and penned up too."

The woman sighed. "Finding two dogs in this wilderness won't be easy, but my husband's a good hunter. He thinks he's only looking for one dog and he won't hesitate to shoot if he sees him."

D.J. felt a sense of panic beginning to seep through his body. "My dog will come back by himself, eventually. But I don't know about the other dog."

"Even if you're telling the truth, and your dog *didn't* bite Roger, it won't make any difference to Bake. That's my husband: His real name's Baker Spinks, but everybody calls him 'Bake.' Anyway, the first dog he finds that looks like your picture is as good as dead."

D.J. looked at Alfred, whose eyes were wide with concern. D.J. said, "Come on, Alfred. Let's go tell my dad what happened."

As the two friends started off across the campground, D.J. groaned. "It's all my fault! If I'd trained Hero better, and if I'd taken him in for his rabies shot, this wouldn't have happened!"

Alfred said, "Don't go beating up on yourself, D.J. What's done is done. We've got to decide what to do now."

"I can't let Mr. Spinks hurt Hero! I just can't!"

"But what can you do?"

"I don't know, but maybe Dad'll think of something. Come on! And say a prayer while we're running!"

* * * * *

When Sam Dillon had listened to what the boys said, he stroked his chin thoughtfully. "I can't let you go out there in the woods with some guy running around with a gun!"

"But, Dad, we've *got* to go look for Hero before that man finds him!"

Dad shook his head. "Too risky, D.J.! You already heard how nasty he sounded when I honked for you boys this morning."

"He wouldn't shoot a person—would he?"

Dad shrugged his huge shoulders. "He didn't look all that upstanding to me, D.J."

D.J. groaned and spun around in anguish just as a forest green car with a white front door and top stopped beside Dad's sedan. Red, amber, and blue lights glistened on the front part of the car's roof. D.J. saw that the front door had the circle emblem of Timbergold County with the familiar words *Sheriff's Patrol.*

" 'Afternoon," the uniformed officer said through the open window. He was a muscular young man with a heavy moustache. His short-sleeved shirt had the two chevrons* of a corporal. The deputy lifted his billed cap and ran tanned fingers through a thatch of thick, black hair. "Everything OK?"

In moments, the deputy had heard the whole story. He got out of his car and stood with the door open. "I know that guy with the tattoos. Baker Spinks. He's a hard case. Our department's had a few

run-ins with him before. You'd better steer a wide
path around him."

"But he'll shoot my dog!" D.J. cried.

"I'll go talk to him," the officer said. "He's hot
tempered, but all he's ever done so far is get busted for
fighting, disturbing the peace, and resisting arrest.
No weapons charges.

"Of course, he shouldn't have a gun in the
campground, but up there where you say he went, it's
OK to carry a weapon as long as it's not concealed.
That's not breaking any laws."

"How about shooting my dog?" D.J. interrupted.

"That's illegal, of course. I'll go have a talk with
him. You boys show me where Spinks went. OK?"

* * * * *

In a couple of minutes, the deputy replaced his
microphone and stepped out of the car. He shoved his
black baton* into the belt ring at his left hip,
adjusted his holstered revolver on his right hip, and
settled the radio handset into place at his belt.

"My name's Brackett," he said, reaching a
muscular bare arm out to shake hands with Sam
Dillon. "Corporal Arlis Brackett." He had a
diamond-shaped shoulder patch on his shirt. He wore
dark brown pants and Wellington boots.

"Sam Dillon," Dad said, shaking hands with the
deputy. "My son's named D.J. and this is his friend,
Alfred Milford. We're from Stoney Ridge."

The boy shook the corporal's hand and started
with him across the campground just as Mrs. Spinks
came hurrying toward them.

"Hey, Officer! My little boy!" she cried, waving
both hands above her head in an excited way. "He

should have been back by now!"

She hurried breathlessly up to the men and boys, pointing toward Devil's Point. "I went partway up the path where he'd gone with his daddy, but I didn't see either of them! I called and called, but Roger didn't answer! Neither did my husband."

Corporal Brackett seemed experienced in dealing with excited and frightened mothers. "These two boys told me what happened, Mrs. Spinks. Don't worry. You know how little kids are. Your son's probably just playing out there in the camp shadows somewhere."

"I don't think so. He was scared of maybe having to take antirabies shots. I'm afraid he ran away!"

The deputy's voice was calm. "I'm sure he'll turn up all right, Mrs. Spinks. But I'll go take a look. OK?"

The woman nodded with relief, and D.J. felt sorry for her. Both she and her husband looked like some people Grandpa Dillon saw once in Indian Springs and said, "They look like old hippies* that don't know that look went out of style years ago."

D.J. looked up at the woman. "We'll find Roger and bring him right back."

She answered softly, "I sure hope so! You see, he's got diabetes.* I give him daily insulin* shots and he hasn't had his injection yet today."

D.J. didn't understand what that meant, but he saw Dad and the deputy exchange looks. Without a word, the two men began hurrying toward the base of Devil's Point. The boys followed, with D.J. sensing that something terrible might be about to happen.

Chapter Three

A THREE-WAY SEARCH

D.J. leaned forward at the waist, puffing a little as he followed his father and the deputy up the mountain trail. Alfred panted in back of D.J. as the sun vanished behind the mountains. Deep shadows silently stole over the two men and two boys. D.J. wanted to ask about diabetes, but the steep trail took all of his breath. The boy knew he couldn't ask his questions until the deputy or Dad stopped.

However, Corporal Brackett and Dad didn't stop until they met four young men with backpacks coming down the trail. D.J. was glad to rest while the four hikers drew close. Then the deputy called out.

"You folks seen or heard a little kid?"

The hikers shook their heads. The deputy asked, "What about a man with a full beard, lots of tattoos, and wearing a holstered sidearm?"

Again, the hikers shook their heads. Corporal Brackett tried once more. "Any sign of a dog?"

D.J. saw the hikers exchange looks. "Yeah," the
tallest young man said, adjusting his pack. "We saw
one on the trail. Mixed breed mutt, brownish
colored, with a stub tail. He didn't make a sound, but
he was sort of staggering."

"Staggering?" The corporal's word exploded into
the still mountains.

"Well, yeah," the leader said, looking at his three
companions. They nodded in agreement. "He was
coming down the trail when we came around a
curve. He seemed sort of strange, so we stepped out of
the way and let him go by."

A hiker with a sunburned nose spoke up. "We
remembered reading the signs about rabies in the
area, and that dog just didn't seem normal. I mean,
he walked a little stiff-legged and unsteady-like. He
had kind of a vacant stare, and didn't even look at us
as he went by."

The deputy adjusted his billed cap on his full head
of hair. "I know our animal control officer says you
can't really tell by looking if an animal has rabies,
but that sure sounds like the symptoms of the 'dumb'
kind."

"Dumb?" D.J. asked without thinking.

Corporal Brackett looked down at the boy. "There
are two kinds of rabies: the furious and the dumb. In
the first, the animal is vicious. In the other, the
animal is quiet. That's the scary kind because kids
sometimes think the animal's sick or hurt or lost,
and they try to pet him. Then he bites them. With the
other kind of rabies, of course, the animal acts so
fierce people automatically get out of his way."

D.J. figured Roger Spinks had gotten bitten

because he tried to befriend the strange dog that looked like Hero. Now the boy was all alone in the wilderness with dusk settling fast.

The officer said, "D.J., show these people the picture of your dog."

The boy removed the photograph from his shirt pocket and held it out. All four hikers glanced at it and nodded. The leader said, "I'd say that's the dog we saw."

D.J. cried out, "That *couldn't* have been my dog!"

The tall backpacker shrugged. "It's hard to say for sure, but I'd say the dog in the picture is the same one we saw back up the trail. Right, guys?"

The other backpackers nodded. D.J. cried out in protest, but the deputy thanked the hikers and stood aside so they could go on down to camp before nightfall.

"Well," Corporal Brackett said with a deep sigh, "that puts a different light on things. It'll soon be dark, so we'd better head back down."

D.J. was frustrated about Hero being unjustly blamed, but there was nothing he could do about it. He asked the question that had been bothering him since he'd first heard the word. "What's diabetes?"

The deputy turned dark eyes on the mountain boy. "It's a disease that impairs the body's ability to use sugar properly. The person usually gets very thirsty and has to go to the bathroom a lot. Diabetes can be controlled pretty well with insulin injections. Trouble is, the disease can be very serious without those shots."

D.J. was afraid to ask, but he had to know. "Could a person die from not getting the shots?"

"Sure could, D.J.," the deputy answered, looking down the trail. "Sure could!"

* * * * *

At the bottom of the trail there was room to walk side-by-side toward the campground. D.J. could see campfires and pressurized lanterns were already fighting to beat back the darkness under the great trees. D.J. walked to the deputy's left with Dad and Alfred on the other side.

Dad rubbed his chin where the day's growth of black whiskers was beginning to make his face look almost blue. "What do you make of all this, Arlis?"

The deputy kept walking, but he lifted his billed cap and scratched his thick head of dark hair. "It's not good. We have to assume the dog that bit the little boy is the same one the hikers saw in their path. We also have to figure that the dog might have rabies."

D.J. protested, "But that can't be my dog!"

"I hope you're right, D.J., but there's no way to prove that at the moment. So I'd better radio in for the animal control officer and the dog handler who takes care of our lost kid cases."

Alfred asked, "What's a dog handler?"

Corporal Brackett chuckled. "He's the man who works with our tracking and scent dogs. We have three of them."

D.J. said, "I know about tracking dogs, but what's a scent dog?"

"Scent dogs pick up human smells in the air while a tracking dog follows a trail. The dog handler never works alone in these mountains. We always send a buddy with him in case something should happen. The animal control officer is what some people used to call a dog catcher."

Alfred said, "D.J.'s going to be an author someday. He could write a story about those tracking and scent dogs."

D.J. had already thought of that, but the deputy didn't seem to have heard Alfred's remarks. The officer continued his explanation.

"As I was saying, we have only three dogs for the whole county. Since Timbergold County stretches from the Mother Lode Gold Country on the west to the Nevada border on the east, we've got a lot of territory and all types of terrain. The land goes from barren foothills less than 1,000 feet in elevation to 10,000 feet above sea level.

"But no matter where a person gets lost, we first call in either the tracking or scent dogs. We also have a search-and-rescue coordinator who organizes volunteer search parties if the dogs fail.

"Usually, we find the lost person the first day. The longest was 46 hours on a lost kid. Thank God, so far we've never failed to find anyone in time to save their lives."

The deputy glanced at the total blackness made by the dense forests growing all around them. He touched the radio handset at his belt. "Even though it'll be pitch black before anyone can get here to start the search, I'd better call in a dog handler. He can work at night."

Dad asked, "Can that little walkie-talkie reach to the sheriff's office?"

Everyone stopped as the deputy paused in an open space where the stars above the treetops were beginning to wink in the evening sky.

"This little radio reaches to the patrol car. They have a portable relay to the dispatcher. This handset can also reach the Tahoe National Forest up on the mountaintop."

D.J. turned away as the deputy began calling on the radio. D.J. was sure Hero would eventually come in by himself, as Dad had said, unless Mr. Spinks caught up to Hero first. But that little lost kid with the dog bite and diabetes was out there somewhere wearing nothing but a pair of cutoff jeans. Even though it was June, the temperature could drop into the 40's at night.

The deputy finished his radio transmission and replaced the handset on his belt. "OK, let's get back to our cars."

As they started walking again, D.J. asked, "How long can that little kid go without his diabetes shot?"

"Insulin shot for diabetes," the deputy corrected. "Depends on the individual case, of course, but I'd guess a day or two; three at the most before it'd be too late. You see, my kid brother had diabetes requiring daily injections. Once he was rafting down a canyon river when he lost his insulin kit. Was without his syringe for two days, and he made it. Just barely, though, because he was almost in a coma by then."

D.J.'s thoughts began tumbling over one another. He couldn't understand how such a simple thing as not having taught Hero to always come when called, or not getting Hero's rabies vaccination could lead to so much trouble.

Yet because of those little failures, Hero was lost in

the high Sierras. An angry father was hunting the dog to kill him because the man thought D.J.'s dog had bitten Roger, and the dog might have infected the boy with rabies. Roger had either run away or gotten lost. He would die if he wasn't found soon.

D.J. didn't want to feel guilty, but all this was really his fault. He had to do something to make it right—but what?

D.J.'s whirling thoughts were interrupted by Corporal Brackett. He stopped as they approached his patrol car. Everyone else stopped too.

"Mr. Dillon, I think the smartest thing for you to do is take D.J. and Alfred back to Stoney Ridge for the night. We're probably going to have our hands full with that hardcase, Spinks, when he comes down. Meanwhile, I'll go over and talk to his wife and see what else I can learn about the situation.

"Much obliged," Dad said softly. "But we'll be back in the morning and bring some friends to help look for the boy and the dogs."

D.J. took a slow, deep breath. That meant Dad wasn't spoiling for a fight with Mr. Spinks. There had been a time when it seemed to D.J. that his father used to go out of his way to get into scraps. Maybe, just maybe, the boy thought, Dad really was changed. But if he wasn't, then he'd get plenty of chance to show it before this mess was over.

Corporal Brackett seemed to be thinking out loud. "The animal control officer can put a call on the local radio stations for volunteers to come help look for the dog that bit Roger. But when the word gets out that they may be looking for a rabid dog, probably not too many people will come.

"As for the lost boy, well, our department likes to let the dogs work alone—except for their handlers—before the trail gets all mixed up with other peoples' tracks and smells. So you folks go on home."

As everyone said goodnight to the deputy and walked toward Sam Dillon's sedan, D.J. looked up past the soaring evergreen trees and the lofty mountain peaks. He didn't want to come back in the morning, or ever; at least, not while the man with the tattoos and the terrible temper was likely to be around. Yet D.J. knew he had to come back to look for his dog.

"Lord," D.J. whispered, "I know it's all my fault, but please let it turn out all right!"

Then D.J. slid into the car with Dad and Alfred, each of them anxious to get home.

* * * * *

It was dark long before Dad and D.J. dropped Alfred off at his home. Then the father and son drove across Stoney Ridge to where three generations of the Dillon family lived in one house. As the car's headlights bounced high from turning into the driveway, D.J. pointed to another car parked against the high curb in front of the neat frame house.

"Oh, good! Brother Paul's here!"

"Sure is," Dad replied as the headlights hit the front porch. "And there's your grandfather, rocking away! Means he's powerful upset about something."

"Because we're so late, I imagine, Dad."

D.J. saw that Grandpa Dillon was rocking very fast in his old red cane-bottom chair. It was going very far forward, then very far back. Usually, that meant the old man would eventually tip over.

He'd fall on the porch and then whang the chair

with his Irish shillelagh.* That's what the old man
called the blackthorn cane he used to ease the pain in
his arthritic hip.

Dad parked in the driveway beside the house. D.J.
leaped out of the car and ran up the front steps before
Grandpa could hurt himself. In the pale glow of the
yellow porch light, Grandpa looked even older than
usual. He stopped rocking. He was a feisty little man
who once had a contrary streak as wide as a barn
door. He was thin as a piece of baling wire and wore
longjohns, even in the summer. His small, round wire-
rimmed bifocals rested far down on his nose.

"Hi, Grandpa!" D.J. cried, stopping in front of the
old man. "We're home!"

"It's about time! You worry a body sick!" The
sharp words exploded into the night. Then Grandpa
sighed and rolled his pale blue eyes upward.
"Thank You, Lord," he whispered.

Grandpa reached out a thin, blue-veined hand
and lightly closed it over the boy's forearm. "I'm sorry
for snapping at you, D.J. Glad you're back. Have car
trouble?"

The boy started to explain when a shriek came
from inside the house, cutting through the screen door.

"Mom! It's *Davey!*"

D.J. winced. He didn't like his nine-year-old
stepsister calling him that. His name was David
Jonathan, but he liked the initials D.J.

In a moment, Pris threw open the sqeaking screen
door and stood looking up at D.J.

Seconds later, D.J.'s stepmother rushed from
inside the house. She was pretty in a slightly plump
sort of way. Her blue eyes showed relief. Her hands

fluttered like frightened birds toward her short blond hair. For a moment, she also stood looking at the boy.

"Hi, Two Mom," he said softly.

"D.J.! You gave us quite a scare! Where's your father? Oh! I see him!" She turned without touching the boy and ran to her husband. "Sam—oh Sam! You were gone so long!"

D.J. didn't get to see what Dad did because suddenly Pris grabbed him and hugged him tight, her face against his chest.

The boy was embarrassed. He looked down at his stepsister. Her dress was neat and clean, but her brown hair looked untidy. It reminded D.J. of an eagle's nest that had fallen on a fence post.

"Hi, Pris," he said, patting her head lightly. Before she could answer, another voice sounded from inside the house. "Kathy, they're here!"

Paul Stagg, the giant lay preacher from Stoney Ridge's only church, pushed the screen door open and flashed a happy grin at the new arrivals. A second later, his daughter appeared.

Kathy was slightly younger than D.J. She had reddish hair like her father, except hers cascaded down both sides of her face like a bright waterfall. D.J. swallowed hard for reasons he couldn't explain. Kathy smiled and the whole porch seemed to light up.

"Hi, D.J."

D.J. replied softly, "Hi, Kathy." He raised his voice and looked around. "Hi, everybody! I'm sure glad to see you all!"

Dad and Grandpa weren't hugging kinds of

people, so D.J. didn't hug much either. Yet he felt such a need for someone to show some real caring.

Brother Paul seemed to sense that. Quickly, he bent and engulfed the boy in his massive arms. When he spoke, his voice seemed like distant thunder.

"D.J., I just feel a powerful need to hug somebody, and you're it!"

The boy was crushed against the man's huge chest. He felt rather than heard the next words that started deep in the big man's chest and rumbled up through that great body as a whisper in the boy's ear.

"I can see it in your face that something bad has happened, D.J. But whatever it is, remember that God'll help you handle it."

D.J. whispered back. "I sure hope so! But it doesn't seem possible right now!"

Chapter Four

A GLIMMER OF HOPE

When D.J. had finished telling what had happened, Grandpa shook his blackthorn walking stick at the ceiling, almost hitting the light fixture.

"I'll find the dog that bit the kid! Then I'll whale the stuffing out of that dog! That's what I'll do!"

Sam Dillon growled, "You'll do no such a thing! You can't go climbing mountains with that bum hip!"

Grandpa bristled, his pale blue eyes snapping with inner fire. "I'll fight Ol' Nick* hisself if he scares my grandson! And don't you nor nobody else try to tell me different!"

For a moment, D.J. thought it was going to be just like it was after Mom died, when Dad and Grandpa argued all the time. Things had been better since Brother Paul Stagg had come to town, and Dad and Pris' mother had gotten married. But D.J. wasn't sure if the arguments between Dad and Grandpa were really gone forever.

The giant lay pracher had been sitting in a large wingback chair, his long legs crossed, his white ten-gallon Stetson hooked over the toe of his top boot. Brother Paul suddenly grabbed his hat and clamped it on his head. He stood quickly, looking nearly seven feet tall. He dropped his huge hands over Dad's and Grandpa's shoulders.

"Now, brothers, Jesus don't like for us to be a'speaking hard-like to each other. Let's just ask the Lord's guidance on finding that little lost boy and the dog that really bit him so D.J.'s dog will be cleared of any blame."

Brother Paul reached up and swept his hat off. He bowed his head and began to pray, softly at first, and then with rising power. D.J. thought Brother Paul prayed better than anyone in the whole world. In fact, D.J. wondered how God could ignore any prayer Brother Paul offered.

When the lay pastor's "Amen" was said and softly echoed by everyone, D.J. raised his head. He quickly glanced around the room. His stepmother smiled at Brother Paul. D.J. saw Two Mom's lips form a silent, "thank you." D.J.'s eyes moved on and caught Kathy looking shyly at him with bright blue eyes from under her cascade of red-gold hair.

The boy's eyes came back to the lay pracher who was still standing.

"Folks," the deep voice rumbled, "if you all got no objections, I'll call my missus and ask her to get the ladies prayer chain a'working on this here problem. Then I'll go home and phone some of the men in the church. Some of them should be able to help search for the dog that bit the little boy."

Grandpa pounded the rubber tip of his cane on the floor. "Brother Paul, you're a man after my own heart! Let's cut out this here palavering* and get crackin',* come first light."

Grandpa eagerly shoved himself to his feet with the aid of his cane, but his arthritic hip betrayed him. He staggered and almost fell.

Paul Stagg reached out a powerful hand and steadied the old man. The lay preacher spoke gently. "Mr. Dillon, sir, I don't mean no disrespect a'tall, but you'd do me and your son and grandson a powerful favor if 'n you stayed here and looked after the womenfolk."

The old man started to protest, but D.J. gripped Grandpa's thin, blue-veined hand with its brown age spots. "Please listen to Brother Paul."

For a moment, Grandpa hesitated. Then slowly he nodded. "Reckon you'uns can handle it out there without me. But keep us posted!"

"We will, Grandpa," D.J. promised. "Now, if nobody minds, I'm going to get some sleep."

"I reckon that's a plumb good idea for everyone," Brother Paul rumbled. "We got a powerful lot of things to do tomorrow morning early."

* * * * *

Dad's gruff voice awoke D.J. before daylight. The boy was still sleepy, but he was also anxious to know if Hero was safe and if Roger had been found. D.J. dressed quickly and joined Dad in the sedan. They stopped to pick up Alfred and reached the Devil's Point Campground at daybreak.

When they neared the gate, D.J. strained to see if Hero had come back. As Dad drove slowly through the gate, D.J.'s eyes went to the undershirt he'd left there yesterday.

Alfred said softly, "Hero didn't come back yet, D.J."

D.J. nodded, too disappointed to speak. Another thought had bothered him through the night: maybe Mr. Spinks had found Hero and shot him.

Dad's voice broke the boy's fearful thoughts. "There's that Deputy Brackett's car and a county station wagon plus the dog pound pickup. But I don't see Brother Paul and the men from church yet."

Arlis Brackett led another uniformed officer plus a man in dungarees* toward the Dillons. Dad got out of the car. D.J. and Alfred followed.

Corporal Brackett said, " 'Morning, Sam, D.J. How are you, Alfred? I know you're anxious to hear, so let me fill you in. No sign of the little boy. I've talked to Spinks, and he didn't find your dog, D.J."

The boy gave a big sigh of relief and grinned at Alfred, who smiled back. Then D.J. remembered the little lost boy. The smile vanished.

The deputy continued, "Spinks is plenty mad, as you can imagine, especially because his son's still missing. Fortunately, his wife's a pretty level-headed woman and she's got him calmed down—at least for the minute. Yet I'd advise all of you to stay away from him because he is unpredictable."

Corporal Brackett paused and indicated his companions. "Oh, I want all of you to meet Dan Hubble and Hank Waymond."

As the handshaking started all around, Corporal Brackett said, "Dan's a deputy like me, but he's also one of the county's three dog handlers. Hank is the animal control officer for Timbergold County. His job is to catch the dog that bit Roger Spinks."

D.J. saw that the dog handler was a younger officer with the build of a weight lifter. His belt had a radio handset and service revolver. He had a pack of some sort that D.J. figured contained survival equipment.

The animal control officer was about six feet tall, wiry, and balding. D.J. had expected him to be in uniform instead of dungarees.

Arlis Brackett explained the day's plans. "We lost valuable time last night because we couldn't get a track or scent dog up here. All three of them were busy on searches on the west side of the county. So this morning Dan will try to find the lost boy, using his dog. Since we never like to send a man out alone, Dan's got a fellow coming in—a civilian who knows the area—to work with him.

"We're also expecting Sal Caldini—he's our search-and-rescue coordinator—to oversee everything. But until he gets here, and so we don't lose any time, I'm acting as coordinator. You volunteers will search for the dog that bit the kid. Since we might be dealing with a rabid animal, I'm sure you know to be very careful.

"Hank, as animal control officer, will figure out where to set his trap. But the most important thing is for Dan to get the scent dog looking for the boy."

Corporal Brackett nodded toward the station wagon. There was enough daylight so D.J. could see a large dog in the back end. The boy didn't recognize the breed though he'd seen similar dogs in films once or twice.

Deputy Hubble, the dog handler, explained. "That's my Rottweiler. Great scent dog. I'll let him out so we can get started."

As the second deputy strode quickly toward the station wagon, the animal control officer spoke up. "I'll have to ask the victim's father where his boy said the dog attack took place. Then I'll decide where to place my trap."

D.J. asked, "You've only got one trap?"

"That's it, D.J. Only got four for the whole county, and the others are in use."

Alfred pushed his glasses up with his right thumb. "I thought you'd use a dart gun."

"Tranquilizer guns are OK if you can get close enough to the animal, but traps work where I may not be. Later, I'll show you how it works. D.J., have you got that picture of your dog? Arlis told me about it, but I've got to have an idea of what the dog looks like so I'll know what I'm looking for."

The boy reached into his pocket and handed the photograph over. "Mr. Waymond, I know my dog didn't bite that little boy."

The animal control officer held the picture close to examine it in the early morning light. "Well, D.J., you may be right. I don't want to get your hopes up, but there is another dog in this area that looks a lot like the one in this picture."

D.J.'s heart leaped with hope. "There is?"

Mr. Waymond tapped the photograph. "Sure is! Trouble is, the man who owns him is an ornery old cuss who lives back down that way." Mr. Waymond pointed across the country road, away from Devil's Point Campground.

"Then let's go see him!" D.J. cried.

"Hold on! Old Man Schmekle's a recluse who is about as friendly as a mother bear with cubs! He ran some backpackers off with a rifle last year when they cut across his property. When the Sheriff's Department went to see Schmekle about the complaint, he threatened our officers too. They called for backup and booked him into the county jail, but the judge let him go with a warning."

Corporal Brackett snapped his fingers. "I remember that case! Hank, if you want to talk to him, you'd better let our department be the lead agency and you come in after we're sure it's safe."

The animal control officer laughed nervously. "You'll get no argument from me on that!"

D.J. was anxious to start, but the second deputy walked up with the Rottweiler on a stout leather leash. "Gentlemen, meet Razzmatazz; Razz for short. OK, Razz, start to work."

The dog started with Sam Dillon and sniffed at his pants legs. Razz moved on to Alfred and then D.J., sniffing each person in turn. D.J. saw that the animal was about two feet high at the shoulders, powerfully built, with short, coarse black hair. He had tan markings on his chest, muzzle, cheeks, and over both eyes. His tail was docked close to his body.

Alfred said, "I've read about these dogs."

The handler smiled. "Is that so?"

"Yes," Alfred said, pushing his glasses up with an unconscious thrust of his right thumb. "They're descended from drover dogs in ancient Rome. From driving cattle there, the dogs crossed the Alps into what is now Germany and a town called Rottweil. They used to pull wagons until they got into police work."

D.J. was proud of his friend's knowledge. In school, kids called Alfred "the Brain," which he didn't like. Right now, D.J. was too impatient to think much about such things.

D.J. asked, "Shouldn't we be out looking, Mr. Brackett?"

"In a minute, D.J. We've got to wait until the dog finishes with us."

D.J. didn't understand. He blinked and looked down at the dog with the broad head and dark brown eyes. He finished sniffing D.J.'s pants leg and turned to Corporal Brackett.

Deputy Hubble, the handler explained, "He's checked each of you out because he knows he's got to find someone who's not here. That's part of his police training because sometimes we don't have an article of clothing from the person we're looking for. However, in this case, I'm sure the mother will have something for us. Well, we'd better go see her and get started looking for the boy."

Just then a sedan, a pickup, and one four-wheel drive vehicle pulled into the campground. D.J. recognized Paul Stagg's car in the lead. As the lights were switched off and men got out, D.J. counted 11 men from church. Since they were going to search for a possible rabid dog, each had brought a club or pick handle.

They all approached the sheriff's units where greetings were exchanged and introductions made. Razz began sniffing each newcomer while Corporal Brackett outlined his plans.

"OK, that's it," he concluded. "Remember to stay

away from where this dog's working so we won't
mess up the little boy's scent. After Razz has had a
chance to start the kid's trail, and Hank's seen where
the dog attack occurred, then you volunteers can start
looking for the dog that bit Roger. Be careful because
it could be a mad dog.

"Mr. Dillon, will you and Alfred show some of
these men where D.J.'s dog took off yesterday? Thanks!
Now, take care of yourselves and come in before
dark. We don't want anyone hurt or lost."

D.J. asked, "What about me?"

Corporal Brackett looked soberly at the boy. "I'm
going to radio for backup, then you can ride with me
when we go check out Old Man Schmekle's place. I
sure hope he doesn't start blasting away at us until we
can find out about his dog."

D.J. swallowed hard and licked his lips which
had suddenly gone dry. "Me too," he said.

Chapter Five

A TERRIBLE DISCOVERY

D.J.'s whole body was jerked about as Corporal
Brackett fought the wheel of his patrol car. It climbed
slowly up a neck-snapping excuse of a road across
the highway from Devil's Point Campground. The faint
tracks led up the steep side of Saddleback Ridge, a
rugged mountainside thick with tall conifers. There
was a well-worn foot trail across the lower center or
"saddle," but so few four-wheel drive vehicles ever
came this way that there really wasn't a road.

D.J. figured Mr. Schmekle must not own a vehicle
or he certainly didn't drive it this way very often. It was
obvious he didn't have visitors drive in either.

Rooster tails of dust rose from two sheriff's units
bouncing ahead of the boy and the corporal. D. J.
twisted his head to look behind. Hank Waymond,
the animal control officer, was barely visible in his
pickup truck because of the choking cloud spewed
up from the three leading patrol cars.

46

Out the side windows, D.J. could see magnificent evergreen trees and black oaks that grew on the mountainsides. It was a beautiful, peaceful looking area, far back from the main roads. It was hard to believe how dangerous this trip might be until the boy again faced forward.

Through the windshield, thick with dust, D.J. saw the two leading cars slow down at a fence line. On both sides of the cattle guard that served as a gate were two hand-lettered signs. Each read:

Keep out!
Or Else!

Corporal Brackett slowed and stopped, letting the dust plume fall away behind him. "OK, D.J., this is as far as you go. Get out and wait for Hank. You'll be safe here while the rest of us go on in. But if you hear any trouble, tell Hank I said for both of you to get out of here and radio for more backup."

D.J. nodded and stepped out into the weed-choked roadway. It was barely more than a trail, with brush growing head-high on both sides. The boy waved to Corporal Brackett. He pulled ahead, following the other two units across the cattle guard and on toward Mr. Schmekle's cabin.

By the time Mr. Waymond's pickup stopped for the boy, D.J. could see the deputies had pulled to a large open area of an acre or two. Trees and weeds had been cleared to form a kind of yard.

There the boy saw a woodpile, a tumbledown corrugated metal shed, and a relic of a windmill with a leaning tank house. A huge pile of dry brush had been gathered in the middle of the open space. The

deputies left their cars and spread out. They walked
past the brush pile.

D.J. thought he heard one of the men call out as
they slowly moved in toward the weathered cabin. It
was barely visible in the shadows of the tall trees at
the edge of the yard.

The boy turned to the animal control officer who
sat behind the pickup's wheel.

"Shouldn't we have heard the dog barking by
now?"

"Yes, if he's there. Personally, I'm glad it is so
quiet. At least the old man's not blasting away at
them."

D.J. tried to feel better. He turned back toward the
cabin. The deputies were out of sight, but a scrub jay
scolded them in harsh tones. An invisible quail
called out in sharp warning cries. Otherwise, all was
serene.

Several minutes passed, then the boy's eyes caught
a movement on the far side of the brush pile. A mother
quail was leading perhaps a dozen marble-sized
chicks from the brush. They ran with amazing speed
for such tiny things. D.J. smiled and pointed.

Mr. Waymond chuckled. "She's trying to sneak
out and into the heavier shelter of the wood where the
men can't see her brood." He paused and then
continued softly, "I don't know why anyone in this
country would let such a bunch of brush pile up like
that. It's a real fire hazard out here in these woods.
That pile should have been burned before the fire
season started."

D.J. looked upward to a high mountain and
pointed. "At least there's a fire lookout station close by.

They'd spot any smoke real fast."

Mr. Waymond leaned down so he could look up where D.J. was pointing. "That's Lobo Peak. Nice older couple spends their summers up there in the fire lookout station, year after year. It's lonely work, but very necessary. You should do a story about them for the paper sometime, D.J."

He started to answer when he caught a slight movement out of the corner of his eye. D.J. swiveled his head to peer at the edge of the timber by the old recluse's shanty. Somebody was moving there, but all D.J. could see was a man's shadow. The boy's heart leaped into full gallop. Then he sighed softly with relief. Corporal Brackett stepped out into the open and walked past the brush pile toward the pickup.

In a moment, the officer stuck his head through the pickup window. "No sign of the dog, but there's evidence he's been here recently. The other deputies are making a quick search of the area in case the dog's nearby. Hank, maybe you should go see if you want to set up your trap around here."

D.J. fought the disappointment that choked his throat. "What about Mr. Schmekle?"

The deputy shook his head sadly. "He's dead."

"*Dead?*" D.J. and Mr. Waymond echoed.

"Been that way a day or so, I'd guess. But we don't know if he died from natural causes or. . . . "

"Or *what?*" D.J. prompted.

"Or from something else."

"Like what?"

The officer hesitated a moment, then answered. "We found signs of a dog bite on his leg."

D.J.'s blood scalded through his body and tingles

of fear raced over his skin, leaving goosebumps everywhere. He asked softly, "You mean maybe he died from rabies?"

The corporal replied, "We won't know the real cause of death until we get a report from the coroner. The old man could have died from something else, like maybe a heart attack. I'd guess he was around 80."

The animal control officer opened his door. "I'll go see about locating the trap here. Will you take D.J. back to camp?"

"Just as soon as I radio in my report. D.J., are you OK? You look a little pale."

"I was thinking about that little lost boy with the dog bite. If the same dog bit him that bit Mr. Schmekle. . . .

The deputy interrupted. "That kid's diabetes problem is more immediate than any possible rabies infection. We've got a few days on that before he absolutely has to start treatment."

D.J. felt guilt wash over him like a giant wave. If anything happened to Roger, it would be D.J.'s fault! And all because of a simple little neglected responsibility to Hero!

* * * * *

It didn't seem to D.J. that things could get worse, but when the corporal had finished radioing in his report, he asked the woman dispatcher, "Any news on the search for the lost boy at Devil's Point?"

"Negative," the female voice from the car speaker was calm and professional. "Twenty-one reported by radio that his scent dog has picked up the child's trail, but no sign of him yet."

The corporal glanced at D.J. and quickly

explained. "Twenty-one is the radio identification number of Dan Hubble, the dog handler."

Corporal Brackett punched his "send" button on his hand-held microphone. He spoke into it. "What about the volunteers searching for the dog that bit the child?"

"Negative. No sightings reported on any dog."

D.J. sighed softly and lowered his head. The driver seemed to understand the boy's emotional pressure. Neither spoke all the way back to the campground. As the officer's patrol unit turned into the gate, D.J. saw that the campground was deserted except for the Spinks' camper.

Corporal Brackett said, "Guess all the campers cleared out for fear there is a rabid dog loose in the area."

Just then Baker Spinks stepped from behind a dense incense cedar and directly into the path of the patrol unit. D.J. felt perspiration suddenly roll down his rib cage.

Corporal Brackett braked the car and whispered, "D.J., you stay here and don't say anything!"

The officer quickly got out of the car, sliding his baton into the ring at his belt. " 'Morning again, Mr. Spinks. How's it going?"

The man glowered at D.J. and kept walking toward the car. The boy swallowed hard as the officer changed directions slightly, blocking the bearded man's way.

Baker Spinks pointed a long finger toward D.J. and snapped, "That kid sitting in your car won't always have you around, Brackett! If my son ain't found soon, or if anything happens to him, you can't protect that kid or his father!"

"Mr. Spinks, are you threatening the Dillons?"

The man didn't answer. He turned abruptly and walked rapidly back across the deserted campground toward the lone remaining camper.

The officer returned to the car, removing his baton. He placed it between the driver's seat and the one where the boy was sitting.

"D.J., I think it might be better if you and your father go back to town. Alfred, the big preacher, and the rest of your friends can carry on the search here until dark."

* * * * *

On the way down to the county seat, D.J. remembered he hadn't written anything for the newspaper all week. The boy didn't relish the idea of telling that to Elmer Kersten, the editor, who owned and published the weekly. Mr. Kersten had long ago made it clear that the first time D.J. missed a deadline, the boy was through as a stringer.

The good smell of newsprint filled D.J.'s nose as he entered the weekly newspaper's front office. Mrs. Haskell, the middle-aged receptionist and bookkeeper, looked up from her metal desk and called a greeting. D.J. waved back but didn't stop. He pushed through the waist-high swinging gate at the end of the counter. D.J. walked through a second door in the rear. Mr. Kersten had an "open door" policy, so his office was open to anyone who wanted to walk in.

The room was small, cramped, and untidy. There was barely room for the editor, his desk and chair, a visitor's chair, several ancient wooden filing

cabinets, and two radio receivers. The one sitting on
the top shelf of an unpainted bookcase was tuned to
the county sheriff's frequency. The receiver on the
second shelf monitored the California Highway Patrol
transmissions. The walls were crowded with award
plaques and aging news photos.

Mr. Kersten sat before an untidy rolltop desk,
editing copy on a tiny section of flat surface where the
clutter had been shoved back. Every pigeon hole in
the desk overflowed with letters and scraps of paper.

The editor was a tall man with shoulders stooped
from many years of leaning over a typewriter. A rim of
pure white hair ran around the back of his head and
above his ears. Otherwise, he was totally bald. He sat
well back from his desk because his stomach had
slipped and stuck out farther than his chest.

He didn't look up or acknowledge the boy's
presence. After a moment, D.J. cleared his throat and
sat down uneasily on a battered metal folding chair
next to the editor's.

"Mr. Kersten," the boy began, "I'm not going to be
able to write anything for you this week. You see,
I've—"

The editor interrupted without stopping his work
or even raising his eyes. His voice was harsh. "D.J., I've
got deadlines to make and a paper to fill. People
expect *news*, not excuses. Now you remember my rule:
If you can't meet your responsibilities, I'll get
someone who will."

D.J. swallowed hard and took a slow breath.
There was that word again: *responsibilities!*

For a moment, the boy sat silently, watching the
editor's quick, sure movements. D.J. wondered how

the small-town newspaper editor could seem to do
two things at once. He worked in an absolute mess. His
cluttered desk was piled high with incredible
amounts of newspapers, stacks of ordinary paper, and
envelopes from which he periodically fished another
press release. After reading the first line, he usually
crumpled the paper and threw it into the waste
basket with a muttered angry comment.

When he did keep a sheet, the editor cut
drastically, omitting whole paragraphs by quick
strokes of a very soft editing pencil. Finally he
stopped and leaned back in his battered old chair that
sqeaked as if it were in pain.

"D.J., I already heard most of your problems from
listening to the sheriff's radio frequency." Mr. Kersten
pointed his pencil at the radio on the top shelf. "I'm
sorry abut the lost boy and your dog. But you're here
and there's nothing you can do for anybody right
now except meet your obligation to this newspaper. So,
even though you're an independent contractor that I
can't order to do anything as I would an employee, I
want you to listen."

D.J. nodded. "I'm listening."

"I'd like you to write a first-person story about the
whole thing, just as it happened. Do some research on
rabies and diabetes and put them in a sidebar."*

D.J. protested, "Mr. Kersten, it's all my fault that
this has happened! I'm so mixed up inside that I can
barely think, let alone write!"

The editor spun back to his editing. The pencil
flew over the sheet. "D.J., have you ever heard that
some editors are about the meanest people alive?"

D.J. had heard that, but he didn't want to admit it.

He didn't say anything.

Mr. Kersten added, "Well, it's true—and I'll tell you what makes us so mean! We've got deadlines to meet, and people bring us junk to print, or want me to write their 'puff'* stories for them! I give the space free; why should I do any more work than necessary?"

The boy didn't say anything, so the editor continued, "Your job as a reporter is to get the facts. Get them *right*, get them *now*, and get them in spite of *anything!* So grab a pencil and I'll tell you what to do."

D.J. took a deep breath. This was the last thing he wanted to do. Yet failing to do what he should have had gotten him into trouble before. The boy reached toward the editor's desk for a pencil and paper.

Chapter Six

D.J. LEARNS SOMETHING STRANGE

A few minutes later D.J. sat at a corner desk by the
light table* in the back shop. He perched on a wooden
stool and sighed as he reached for the telephone. D.J.
hadn't expected the editor's actions, and would much
rather have gone home. However, he had no choice.
He dialed the veterinarian who once treated Hero, the
boy's scruffy hair-pulling bear dog.

"Dr. Linden, this is D.J. Dillon. You treated my
little dog one time when he had a foxtail* in his ear."

"What can I do for you, D.J.?"

"I'm calling from the *Timbergold Gazette*. I need
to know about rabies. Can you help me?"

"Probably. Something wrong?"

D.J. explained. The vet listened silently and then
replied. "I once had to take those shots myself."

"You got bitten?"

"Actually, no. We had a hog with a condition we
couldn't diagnose."

"Pigs can get rabies?" D.J. asked.

"Any mammal can, including bats. In the hog's case, I'd been handling it during the course of an examination, of course. When the animal died, we naturally suspected rabies. So we had the brain flown by helicopter to Berkeley for laboratory examination."

"Helicopter?"

"Because of the time element, I couldn't wait the usual four days or so for the lab report. So even though Timbergold County Sheriff's Department had no helicopter, they got the highway patrol's chopper to help us. When the report came back that the tests were positive, I took the shots as a precaution."

"Even though you hadn't been bitten?"

"Even though I hadn't been bitten."

"Was it painful, Dr. Linden?"

"Nothing compared with the old ones. But you should ask a physician about that, or maybe the county health officer."

"I'll do that in a minute. Dr. Linden, can a person tell by looking whether an animal has rabies?"

"Usually not. Oh, an animal might stagger, or seem to have a vacant stare, but basically, I'd say it's almost impossible to tell visually."

"What about foaming at the mouth and that sort of thing?"

"On a warm day, or if the animal's just been drinking water, people might see some slobbering and mistake that for signs of rabies. Actually, salivation is a false clue. I'd say it's next to impossible to visually determine if an animal is rabid."

"So the best thing is to stay away from unknown animals?"

"Absolutely! Especially any that behave strangely. Incidentally, when I was a boy, people called dogs with rabies 'mad' dogs or said they had hydrophobia. That means 'fear of water.' Actually, a rabid animal can't drink because he can't close his jaws right. Of course, they can and *do* bite—usually anything that gets in their way."

D.J. thanked the veterinarian and dialed the number of Dr. Nekton, the Dillon family doctor. His receptionist said the doctor was just finishing up an emergency case and would call D.J. back. The boy hung up and dialed Warren Dobbler, the county health officer.

When D.J. had identified himself, Mr. Dobbler's voice was warm and friendly over the phone. "I see your byline on stories from Stoney Ridge, D.J. What are you doing here in Indian Springs?"

D.J. explained. The health officer's voice changed to seriousness. "How can I help?"

The boy began asking questions. His pencil skated over the paper. As the editor had told D.J. some time ago, a good reporter would learn to write almost as fast as a person talked. Finally the boy finished his notes and laid his pencil down to work his cramped right fingers.

"Let me read those back to you, please, Mr. Dobbler. The old rabies shots were called 'duck embryo,' and the new one is called 'human diploid cell vaccine.' "

"Right, D.J. That's a post-exposure immunization. A doctor would now give five shots in the arm compared with twenty-five in the abdomen of the old-type treatment. Also, if it's confirmed as a rabies case, one dose of rabies immune globulin is now also given. This is more passive; the others are more active."

D.J. wanted to have a fuller explanation, but he was also in a hurry. He read from his notes.

"You said this county gets several hundred reported animal bites each year, but it's been years since anybody's died from rabies in this whole country. None would have died if they'd had the vaccine. Right?"

"I'd have to look it up to be sure, but that's my impression; yes."

"Going on: rabies virus gets into the nerve trunks and travels to the brain and spinal cord, then back down to all the nerves. The victim gets paralyzed and eventually dies, if not treated."

"You take good notes, D.J."

"There are two kinds of rabies: the *furious*, where the dog or animal is vicious and aggressive. In the *dumb* type, the process seems to skip the furious stage. Yet the virus is equally dangerous in either the furious or the dumb type rabies."

D.J. didn't want to ask, but he had to know. "How can you tell if an animal is rabid?"

"Well, the suspected animal may be penned up for observation. If there's reason to believe the animal has rabies, then the lab is involved."

"How's that done?"

"The only safe way is to have the animal's brain examined for the virus."

D.J.'s heart leaped with pain, thinking of someone

doing that to Hero. The boy asked, "Isn't there any other way?

"There's a less reliable test where a hair follicle from a living dog or suspected animal is used, but that's not allowed in California."

D.J. thanked Mr. Dobbler and quickly hung up. The boy's chin sank upon his chest. If that happened to Hero, D.J. would never get over it. It would all be D.J.'s fault! But if the dog that bit the little boy was really Mr. Schmekle's, then that dog would have to be examined for the hydrophobia virus. That is, if Brother Paul's volunteers or Hank Waymond, the animal control officer, could catch him.

D.J. raised his head and tried to get his mind back on the work at hand. He still had a long list of questions Mr. Kersten had asked. D.J. needed to call the sheriff's office to find out how a mountain search-and-rescue operation was carried out if the scent dog failed to find the lost person.

The boy reached for the phone again when the editor walked in. "D.J., most of the county offices close at 5 o'clock. You'd better call it a day."

"But I'm not through with the questions you gave me, Mr. Kersten. I've got a call in to Dr. Nekton to ask about diabetes, and I was just going to. . . . "

The editor interrupted. "They'll keep! I've got an early dinner meeting in Stoney Ridge. Come on. I'll give you a ride home."

As D.J. rose to go, the phone rang. The editor answered it and handed it to D.J., saying, "It's the doctor returning your call."

"Thanks, Mr. Kersten." D.J. took the phone. He tried to sound like a reporter. "Hi, Dr. Nekton. Thanks for calling me back. I'm doing a story for the newspaper and need some medical facts about diabetes. Yes, I know I'm young, but I'm sure Mr. Kersten will let me show you what I've written before it's printed so there won't be any mistakes."

The boy glanced up at the editor who nodded. D.J. turned his eyes to the paper and began to write again. Mr. Kersten looked over his shoulder.

When the boy had hung up, he sat silently looking at the notes for a long minute. Then he spoke in a soft, scared voice.

"The doctor says that if that little boy is taking daily insulin injections, and this is the second day without them, then Roger's got to be found by tomorrow for sure, or it probably will be too late. Maybe it already is."

The editor cleared his throat. He spoke gently, the blunt hardness softened. "Everyone's doing all that can be done to find him, D.J. Dan Hubble, the dog handler, will continue searching through the night. I heard that on the sheriff's radio frequency a few minutes ago.

"I also heard the California Highway Patrol say they'll make their new helicopter available if the boy needs to be evacuated to a hospital fast. So it'll be OK, D.J."

He wasn't sure. Sitting on the high stool, the boy slumped forward. He felt the editor's hand lightly touching his shoulder.

"D.J., maybe it wasn't your dog that bit that boy. It wasn't your fault the little kid ran away or got lost, either."

D.J. raised eyes that felt hot and scalding in his

head. "But if I'd made sure Hero had gotten his rabies shots, then they wouldn't even suspect him!"

"That's true, but it wouldn't change the fact that the boy was bitten by a dog that might be rabid. It wouldn't change the fact that the child has severe diabetes. None of that is your reponsibility, D.J."

The boy slowly stood up. "That doesn't help the way I feel. If I'd done what I should have with Hero, I wouldn't be in this mess."

"Stop it!" The editor's voice took on his usual blunt tone. "Guilt is a terrible thing for anyone to carry around, especially a boy your age. You've got to stop thinking about what you should have done and decide what you can now do, if anything. Come on; I'll take you home."

Mr. Kersten turned on the night-lights and set the burglar alarm. He led the way out the back door which he locked. D.J. followed the editor to the carport where he kept his little foreign-made sedan. As they got into the car, D.J. had a thought.

"Mr. Kersten, could you drop me off at the Stoney Ridge Community Church on the way?"

"Sure, but I doubt anybody'll be there this time of day."

"That's OK."

For a moment, the editor seemed about to say something. Then he nodded and inserted the key into the ignition. "Want me to wait for you there?"

"No, but would you mind calling my folks and telling them where I am? Tell them I'll walk home; it's not far."

"Be glad to, D.J."

The editor backed the car out into the alley and

headed away from Indian Springs toward Stoney
Ridge. D.J. glanced at the sky. To the east, the
thunderheads were beginning to form. To the west,
the sun was dipping fast over Stoney Ridge. Soon it
would be night—maybe the last night on earth for
the lost boy.

D.J. sank miserably down into the editor's front
seat. Waves of doubt and fear tried to smother D.J.
The weight seemed about to crush him as the car
wound down the mountain road. Desperately, the boy
thought, *There must be something I can do! But
what?*

He hoped the answer would come to him in the
little frame church.

Chapter Seven

A STILL, SMALL VOICE

The little church stood like a gleaming white spot of hope on the darkening hillsides. D.J. had a good feeling as Mr. Kersten turned into the paved parking lot and stopped under one of the stately ponderosas.

The editor said softly, "Something peaceful and beautiful about an old country church, isn't there, D.J.?"

The boy nodded but didn't answer. He was hurting too much to trust his voice. He got out of the car, silently waved to Mr. Kersten, and waited while the editor drove away. D.J. looked thoughtfully at the church.

It was a tiny frame building with a few very old gravestones in back where members had been buried before a larger community cemetery was begun across town. The church's presence seemed to guard the past and the future while offering hope for the present.

The corrugated metal roof had once been silvery, but now it was rusted with the melting snows of many winters. Thousands of woodpecker holes in the open bell tower looked as though someone had repeatedly hit it with double-ought buckshot.* The heavy bell hung mutely waiting for someone to pull the long rope and call the people together. D.J. had sometimes rung that bell on Sunday mornings.

The boy's blue eyes lifted toward the small white cross glistening on top of the belfry. Even in the gathering dusk, the cross seemed to point up to God, down to the church, and out to the world.

D.J. walked slowly past the evergreens by the front door. He stopped at the foot of the worn wooden steps. The double doors, shrunken with hot weather, had pulled away enough so that the boy could see the metal tongue of the lock.

With a groan of despair, D.J hurried onto the little covered porch and tried the door, just to be sure. It attled loosely but didn't open.

Why should God's house be locked? D.J. cried inwardly. *Who'd steal from Him? I want in!*

He shook the door harder. The lock slipped free with a sharp click. D.J. blinked. The wooden frame hadn't given way; the door had just popped open. D.J. opened it slowly and stepped inside.

It was dark and smelled of old things. It was full of memories too; some good, some bad. When D.J. was a baby, his mother had brought him here. Over the years, D.J. had attended Sunday School here with her, though Dad and Grandpa Dillon didn't attend church in those days.

Yet, sometimes the Dillon family had come here

together. That had been mostly for weddings and
funerals. D.J. had come with his family when Mr.
Higgins had been killed in a logging accident. D.J.
had watched Mrs. Higgins and her little girl, Priscilla,
as the people mourned with them. Later, funeral
services for D.J.'s own mother had been held in this
church. More recently, Mrs. Higgins had become
D.J.'s stepmother in a wedding ceremony performed
here.

For awhile, the church had been closed because
there was no pastor for such a small community. Then
Brother Paul Stagg had come and reopened it as a
lay preacher. From the pulpit, he had once called for a
moment of silence when it was thought D.J.'s little
dog, Hero, had given his life to save the boy and Kathy,
the big preacher's daughter, from an outlaw bear.

More recently, Grandpa Dillon had made his
Christian commitment here. Soon after that, Sam
Dillon had also surrendered his life to the Lord. Now
the whole family came regularly to worship in this little
island of peace and hope called a church.

In joy or in sadness, there was something special
about this sacred spot. Right now, D.J.'s pains were so
deep he knew that this was where he wanted to be.

He thought he was too old to cry, but his eyes
became hot coals in his head. Soon he felt scalding
tears that he refused to let out. They misted across
his eyes and blurred his vision. Barely able to see, he
almost stumbled past the few pews with their high
wooden backs. He stopped before the curving altar at
the front of the church.

D.J. dropped heavily into the front row and stared
silently ahead for a moment. The American and

Christian flags stood in the left corner behind the plain wooden pulpit. A handmade redwood cross hung comfortingly against the wall between the two slender windows behind the high-backed chairs on the raised platform.

Through the windows, D.J. could see the beautiful ponderosa trees on the mountainsides beyond Stoney Ridge. There was no wind, so the trees stood silently, their narrow tops pointing mutely toward the sky.

The boy's eyes came back to the pew. He picked up a *King James Version* of the Bible from the tufted cushion. Slowly, he turned the pages, seeing familiar words, but nothing that made him want to stop and reread them.

Suddenly, D.J. wondered, *Responsibility! What does the Bible say about that?*

He flipped to the small concordance in the back. He skimmed the right page. "Respecteth, respite, rest— *responsibility* isn't there?"

The boy got up and went behind the curving altar to look underneath the pastor's lectern. D.J. knew Brother Paul kept a regular concordance there. Holding the book up to the light from the back windows, D.J. checked again.

The word *responsibility* did not appear in the *King James* concordance. What could that mean? Surely God required people to be responsible.

There must be another word for it—a synonym, the boy told himself as he replaced the concordance and walked back to the front pew. As D.J. tried to think what the synonym might be, he picked up the Bible again.

It seemed to open at a page where someone had underlined a verse in ink. D.J.'s eyes automatically read the words:

To him that knoweth to do good, and
doeth it not, to him it is sin (James 4:17).

D.J. knew that his not having taken care of getting Hero's shots and license was his fault, but was it more than that? Was it a sin against God? After all, D.J. had known what he should have done, and yet he hadn't done it.

He didn't intend to kneel. He slipped from the front seat to his knees. He gripped the altar, subconsciously feeling the chips and scars in the wood. Yet somehow these even felt right to the boy's touch. His head bent forward, the yellowish-blond hair spilling over his forehead and onto the altar.

No words came. D.J.'s anguish was too great for such things. His mind alone cried out in silent petition. Vaguely he remembered that there was some scriptural promise about the Holy Spirit making intercession with groanings that could not be uttered. Brother Paul had once explained that was when you wanted to pray but couldn't, or didn't have the words.

D.J. had no idea how long he was there, still as a stone. At last he raised his head. It came up slowly as though in doubt. Then it rose higher and his moist face tipped upward to the ceiling. Night had come. The church interior was bathed in soft, warm shades of darkness that held no fear and no threat.

Abruptly, D.J. got to his feet. For a moment, he hesitated, his eyes probing beyond the altar, past the redwood cross, through the two small windows on

the back wall behind the pulpit. The sun had set,
but there was just enough light on the horizon to make
silhouettes of the Christmas-tree shaped evergreens
on the hillsides. The conifers nodded slightly in the
evening breeze, somehow seeming to confirm the
boy's thoughts.

He turned and hurried out the door. He closed it
automatically and heard it click into place. He jerked
at it and bent in the soft darkness to make sure it was
again locked. He couldn't see the metal tongue, but
when D.J. shook the doorknob, the lock rattled
securely in place.

D.J. turned, shouted aloud, and ran through the
night toward home. He could hardly wait for morning.

* * * * *

Shortly after dawn, D.J. leaned forward as his dad
turned the sedan into Devil's Point Campground.
It was deserted except for the Spinks' camper and a
sheriff's patrol unit parked inside the grounds.

The boy's eyes immediately went to his old
undershirt. It was still where he'd left it against the tree
stump, but there was no sign of Hero. For a
moment, the good feeling D.J. had felt the night before
threatened to give way to doubt, but the boy shook
the thoughts away.

Dad pulled up alongside Corporal Brackett's
patrol car. The officer slid out of his seat and stepped
over to the Dillons' vehicle. Dad and D.J. got out to
greet him.

"Any news?" D.J. asked quickly.

"Sorry, D.J. I just talked with our dog handler on
his handset. The Rottweiler's still searching, but it's
very rugged country and we're about out of time for

that little kid."

Dad nodded. "Any news on the dog that bit him?"

"No, not yet. Nothing on your dog, either. Hank Waymond, the animal control officer, told me late yesterday that he had set a trap up at Schmekle's cabin. But when Hank went to check it just before dark last night, he'd caught a raccoon."

D.J. asked, "How'd he do that?"

"It's a problem with those traps, D.J. You see, they're the humane kind: sort of a wire box with one end open. There's a spring-loaded door so it falls of its own weight and locks when an animal enters and steps on the trigger. But, of course, all kinds of varmints go after the bait."

"Does the trap hurt them?" D.J. asked.

"No, not at all. So Hank let the 'coon out and reset the trap with some dry dog food. He'll go check it again this morning."

A four-wheel-drive vehicle turned into the campground and eased up behind Corporal Brackett and the Dillons.

Corporal Brackett said, "Oh, here comes our search-and-rescue director, Sal Caldini. He came in yesterday afternoon from another case up north. I don't think you've met him."

Sal Caldini was a dark complected man with a bald head and a huge black moustache that fell below the corners of his mouth. He wore blue jeans and a yellow T-shirt. He carried a large map partly folded under his left armpit.

When introductions had been made, D.J. cleared his throat.

"Mr. Caldini, the *Timbergold Gazette* editor told

me to check with you about some scientific ways
you've learned to do search-and-rescue work."

Dad said softly, "Not now, D.J.!"

"It's important, Dad. Please let me ask him a few
questions."

Mr. Caldini said, "It's OK with me if you'll ride
along while I take care of some things."

D.J. looked at his father who nodded. Dad and
Corporal Brackett walked away talking. D.J. got into
the front seat of the four-wheel-drive vehicle and Mr.
Caldini took the wheel.

The boy turned to the dark-eyed man and said, "I
thought you'd be in uniform like the other deputies."

Mr. Caldini smiled as he swung his vehicle
around and headed for the highway.

"Actually, I'm a civilian who trains people in
search-and-rescue techniques more than actually
doing it myself. Of course, I've been all over the
country on countless cases, but now I mostly teach
others how to do it right."

"Does it work?"

"So far, in every case where we've used the system
I recommend, we've found the lost person alive."

D.J.'s heart leaped with hope. "You mean there's
still a chance to find that little lost boy in time?"

"I hope so, D.J., because that's why I'm here."

"What about the scent dog?"

"He's got his job, and does it well. But my work is
different. Here, take this map and I'll explain it to you
as we drive."

D.J. took the map and unfolded it on his lap as the
vehicle turned onto the highway and began climbing
toward Lake Tahoe. D.J. had never seen a map like

it before.

Then a shadow fell across the map. The boy glanced up. Thunderheads were spreading out along the top of the mountains and blotting out the morning sun. The storm was moving in fast. When it hit, all chances of the scent dog finding Roger Spinks would be lost.

Chapter Eight

A SEARCH-AND-RESCUE EXPERT

Mr. Caldini said, "You're holding a topographic map. Those contoured lines you see show the features of this area. Notice also that there are peaks, ranges, trails, rivers, and other details."

D.J. glanced at the map and nodded. "This is great! But how will it help you find a lost person?"

The search-and-rescue coordinator peered out the windshield at the rising thunderheads. "Well, nature's always a problem in such cases, of course. Not only the land, but the weather."

He eased off the highway at an overlook area. It was so early in the morning no other cars had stopped. The man and boy got out and walked toward the guard rail above the highway.

"You see, D.J., except in the case of a track or scent dog where only two people are involved—the dog handler and his buddy—it's really kind of dumb to just go charging off in the woods when we receive a missing person report. But people get worried and excited—especially when there's a little lost kid—and emotions make the people want to just start searching right away."

D.J. looked across the peaceful-looking mountains and said softly, "That's what I'd do."

Mr. Caldini shook his head. "It's important to ask questions first. In fact, I've worked out almost 250 questions that should be asked before anybody starts off except for the dog handler and his assistant."

"Isn't that a waste of time?"

"I don't think so. The more information we can gather early-on about the missing person, the better chance we have to find him. From statistical probabilities, based on thousands of searches across the country, we know a lot about what a lost person is likely to do."

"Oh?"

"For example, a lost person generally travels downhill because it's easier. However, in the case of a hunter, he'll often set out across country while a fisherman will tend to stick to the streams."

"But what about that little lost boy?"

"Three-fourths of the time, when a kid is over six years old, like this Roger Spinks kid, he won't go more than four miles downhill or two miles uphill."

D.J. looked at the panorama spread out below. "You mean that little kid is almost surely somewhere within two to four miles of here?"

"Very little doubt at all, D.J., though once we found one who'd traveled nearly seven miles. What I wish people, especially kids, would do when they realize they're lost is just sit down and wait. Pick a tree—trees are friendly—and stay with it. We'll find them if they stay put.

"As for the questions: well, maybe one witness saw the victim over to the west, and we start the search there. But if we'd asked enough questions, maybe we'd find another witness who had seen the person later, and that was to the east. By asking enough questions—and the right ones—we save valuable time. We keep asking questions, even as we're looking. A good place to do that is at trail heads where hikers come in from various directions. That way, we keep narrowing our options down until we can pinpoint the most likely area where the lost person is to be found."

"Then you use this map?" D.J. guessed.

Mr. Caldini took the map from the boy and spread it out on the flat guard rail. "Look at the map and then follow where I point and you'll see how well it works.

"See Devil's Point there with the campground below by the road? Across that highway we have Lobo Mountain rising up steeply with a pass through it called Saddleback Ridge. Lobo Peak Fire Lookout Station is there to the left. Off to the east is Lake Tahoe where those storm clouds are building up. Sacramento's to the west in the valley."

D.J. was surprised how easy it was to read the topographic map. He could make out everything Mr. Caldini mentioned. D.J. was studying only a few square miles on the map, but the area was rugged and primitive with lots of brush and timber. Hero was in there somewhere. So was another dog that likely had rabies, and looked like Hero.

Mr. Caldini spoke again. "We're limited in asking questions because so many people left when they heard about a possible rabid dog in the area. So I drove up here to take a look at the whole place and compare it with my topographic map before making an educated guess where the boy might be. I'd say the scent dog's working in the wrong area."

D.J. frowned. "You mean the Rottweiler's not following Roger?"

"Oh, that dog's on the scent, all right. But I have a feeling he's behind because the boy didn't get lost up where his father last saw him."

D.J.'s frown deepened. "He didn't?"

"No, I believe the boy came back to camp, crossed the highway toward Lobo Mountain, away from Devil's Point."

"Why would he do that?"

"From the questions I asked his mother, I learned Roger was scared about taking rabies shots. I guess his father didn't know the new type isn't so painful as the old ones given in the abdomen. Roger threatened to run away. That would logically mean going up or down this highway, either toward Sacramento or up to Lake Tahoe. Then he got lost; not before."

"But wouldn't someone have seen him if he was on the highway? I mean, he's so little!"

"Someone *did* see him. I found that out in asking questions. The California Highway Patrol had a report of a little kid walking along the roadway toward Lake Tahoe."

"What happened?"

"When an officer got there, there was no sign of the child."

D.J. frowned in thought. "Roger could have been picked up by someone, or kidnapped, or even hurt and left by the side of the road."

"Or he could have taken off into the brush."

"Why would he do that?"

"He might have seen the CHP unit and hid because he was afraid. Or maybe he found an easy trail or road that looked interesting. Like that one."

D.J. followed where Mr. Caldini pointed. "I've been on that one," the boy said. "That leads up Lobo Mountain and over Saddleback Ridge to Mr. Schmekle's place!" D.J. turned to look at Mr. Caldini. "Could that little boy have gone this way?"

"Yes, he could have, of course. But if there were more people to ask questions, maybe I could give you a better answer. However, we're running out of time. If that storm hits, it'll wash out the boy's scent. It'll be too late to get enough volunteers in here for a ground search."

He turned back toward his vehicle. D.J. followed.

"So what're you going to do?"

"I'd like to ask more questions from hikers and others so I could pinpoint the boy's probable location. Get in. I'll take one last look and then I'll have to call for more deputies and volunteers to help search this area."

D.J. slid into the passenger's side and buckled his seat belt. "Will they start before that storm?"

"No, unfortunately. They can't do much in lightning storms. But we can't afford the delay, either."

"I'm glad I don't have *your* job, Mr. Caldini."

"It's hard. If I guess wrong, that kid dies. But if I figure things right, he'll live. Thank God, so far we haven't lost a single life. I just pray this boy turns out to be another one of those lucky ones."

D.J.'s eyes swept the mountainous terrain again as Mr. Caldini backed up and pulled out of the overlook area. He checked the highway and drove onto it, heading back toward the campground.

D.J. said, "When we get back to the campgrounds, let me off, please. I hope my best friend is there now. Maybe some men from our church too. They're helping my Dad look for my dog."

"Sure thing, D.J. But I'm going to stop first and ask those hikers up ahead if they've seen or heard anything."

D.J. saw four young men just coming out of the timber. They'd followed the trail the boy had seen on the map, the trail that ran over Saddleback Ridge and down Lobo Mountain.

As the vehicle slowed, D.J. asked, "Mr. Caldini, from your map, would you say it would be easy for a dog to go from the campground up Lobo Mountain and over Saddleback Ridge?"

"If you're talking about Old Man Schmekle's dog—I heard about that situation when I was asking questions—I'd say it would depend. If his dog is normal, it would be natural for him to follow that trail back and forth—from the campground to his home. But if he's rabid, then logic goes out the window and there's no telling where he would travel."

The vehicle stopped on the shoulder and Mr. Caldini got out to approach the hikers who were almost to the roadway. D.J. opened his door and jumped to the ground. He was thinking it wouldn't hurt to walk up Lobo Mountain toward Saddleback

Ridge to whistle and call for Hero in case the dog crossed the road.

Mr. Caldini seemed to read the boy's thoughts. "If you're thinking of looking for your dog alone and on foot, I'd forget it. Assuming your dog's OK but that Schmekle's dog may be rabid, you'd be in a lot of trouble if you ran across him out there all by yourself."

"But maybe he's not really rabid. Maybe he's just mean."

"*Maybe*, but I wouldn't risk it, D.J. Wait a minute and I'll take you back to your father. You can go with him and your friends."

"Well, thanks, but it's not far back to camp. I'll just walk."

"Suit yourself. Well, good luck, D.J." The search-and-rescue man began walking toward the young men with backpacks coming out of the timber.

D.J. shaded his eyes and studied the mountains around him.

I wish Alfred were here, D.J. thought. *We'd go up that old road a little way and see if there's any sign of that little kid. Maybe we'd find my dog too. But from the looks of those clouds, by the time I found Alfred and we. . . .*

D.J.'s thoughts snapped off. Baker Spinks was just walking out of Devil's Point Campground. D.J. recognized the leather hat, the wild beard, and the big holstered pistol at his hip.

The mountain boy ducked behind an incense cedar growing by the roadside. D.J. peeked around enough to see that Mr. Spinks was coming his way. D.J. slid back behind the cedar, his mind whirling.

Carefully, D.J. moved away, bending nearly double to stay out of sight. Then he stopped dead still, listening. A dog barked sharply in the distance.

"Hero!" the boy breathed aloud. "That's Hero!"

D.J. forgot Mr. Spinks and scrambled up the steep hillside toward Saddleback Ridge. He strained to hear his dog bark again. Instead, he heard the first faint rumble of thunder as the storm approached. Then D.J. glanced behind him. Mr. Spinks had seen him!

"Hey, you! Kid! Wait!"

D.J. scurried up Lobo Mountain so fast he slipped and fell. He leaped up at once and glanced back. The bearded man was chasing after him, running hard up the mountainside!

Chapter Nine

A GHOSTLY CHASE

D.J.'s chest seemed about to burst before he stopped to rest in the dense shade of a ten-story-tall Douglas fir. Lobo Mountain was steep and filled with small ravines, downed logs, huge granite boulders, dense underbrush, and towering conifers.

As D.J. tried to control his tortured breathing, he stared back down the way he had come. There was no sign of Mr. Spinks, but that didn't mean he had turned back. In fact, he was almost surely still chasing D.J.

The boy desperately wanted to whistle and call for his dog, but he didn't want Mr. Spinks to know for sure where he was. So the boy listened, sucking in great, ragged gulps of air. Then he ran again, keeping to the shadows of the great trees so Mr. Spinks couldn't easily see him.

There was no doubt D.J. was hearing Hero's sharp bark, yet it was hard to tell where the sound was coming from. The mountains and canyons echoed the sound so it seemed to come from every direction. Yet the boy sensed it was higher up on Lobo Mountain, maybe even beyond Saddleback Ridge.

There was something different about Hero's bark, D.J. decided. It wasn't the bark the little dog made when answering D.J.'s call. It wasn't the hair-puller's baying voice he used when running a trail. Neither was it a "treed" bark. It was more like the bark Hero used when he was tied up and wanted to be free.

The boy checked behind him from the safety of a huge granite boulder. Shadows were moving below him, but they could have been from a person or just the fast-moving clouds that were threatening to blot out the sun. D.J. figured the bearded man was trying to stay out of sight until he was upon D.J. Maybe Roger's angry father would even try to circle around and get ahead of D.J. so he'd run right into him, all alone, out in the wilderness.

D.J. listened. He couldn't hear Mr. Spinks. Hero had stopped barking. "Must be down in a canyon or behind a mountain. I wonder if Mr. Spinks hears him, or if he just saw me?"

The boy thought about stopping long enough to see if he was still being followed, but decided against it. He lifted his eyes to the sky. The thunderheads were spreading out overhead. They were losing their beautiful white puffiness. Instead, they were taking on a dark gray color with tinges of black.

The boy went on until he came to a set of tire tracks. He bent to examine them. Fairly fresh. D.J. stood up and looked around. "Of course! This is the road the deputies took when we drove up to Mr. Schmekle's cabin!"

D.J. followed the tracks because the going was easier, and it'd take him over Saddleback Ridge. In one small area, melting spring snows had carried a stream of sand and fine dust across the tire tracks. Animal paw prints had already been made on top of the tire tracks.

D.J. bent to take a close look. A raccoon had left prints that reminded D.J. of a human baby's hand print. A skunk had dragged its thick bushy tail across the sand. Neat, dainty cloven hooves showed where a deer and her fawn had passed. But there were no human footprints.

The boy straightened up and went on, feeling good that he could recognize most tracks the way he could tell one letter of the alphabet from another.

In the distance, Hero barked again, causing D.J. to stop abruptly and listen. Then the boy caught a glimpse of movement. Mr. Spinks was just topping a bald granite dome slightly ahead and off to the right. Somehow he had outclimbed D.J.

For a moment, the boy hesitated. It was a rule of forest safety never to leave a trail. That's what got people lost. Still, D.J. felt sure of his ability to find his way back. Besides, he couldn't risk running into the man with the gun. D.J. slipped quietly off the trail into the underbrush.

Almost immediately, the boy saw he was heading toward dense clumps of poison oak. He stopped, looking for a way around.

"Got to risk going down a little to get around that stuff," D.J. told himself. Bending low and trying to keep his pursuer from seeing him, D.J. quickly and quietly retraced his steps. When he came to the sandy spot where he'd seen the raccoon and skunk tracks, the boy stopped dead still.

He stared in disbelief, then bent to make sure. "Dog tracks! They weren't here a minute ago!"

They were about the same size as Hero's, but the boy could still hear the little hair-puller barking away off in the distance. These tracks had to be from the dog that bit the little boy!

The realization snapped D.J. upright again. He turned quickly, spinning in a circle, his blue eyes skimming over the heavy underbrush. He tried to see into the deep shadows of the dense stands of evergreen trees.

Nothing! Yet the boy knew the dog had to be close by, watching him. The animal must have deliberately left the trail when it heard the boy coming back.

The short hair on the back of D.J.'s neck started to crawl. Goosebumps ran down his shoulders, across his arms, and down to his wrists. He had been scared enough about Mr. Spinks following him. But D.J. got a spooky feeling knowing that a dog was sneaking up on him. It was like being chased by a ghost.

The boy looked around for a stick or club, but there wasn't a thing close by. Off in the shadows of the pines and oaks and cedars, dead limbs lay scattered about. D.J. decided it wasn't wise to go into the shade now being made deeper by the clouds hiding the sun.

The boy debated with himself. *Should I try to slip back to camp or should I try to find the dog, especially with Mr. Spinks close by?*

Hero's bark came again. D.J. decided. He headed
into the brush, circled the poison oak away from where
he'd seen Mr. Spinks, and moved uphill toward the
pass through Lobo Mountain.

D.J. found a stout limb that had fallen from a
ponderosa. D.J. scooped up the stick in his right hand
and tested it against his open left palm. It wouldn't
do any good at all if Mr. Spinks caught him, and it
wouldn't help much against a determined dog. Still,
the stick gave D.J. a sense of security.

He went on, climbing steadily toward where he'd
heard his dog. D.J.'s head turned constantly. He
checked in every direction for signs of the ghostly
dog that was following him, silent as a shadow; or of
the man with the gun.

But what if Mr. Spinks had now gotten far enough
ahead and was waiting for D.J.? What if the strange
dog had also circled around and was waiting in
ambush for D.J. ahead? What if when he was climbing
over a downed log or pushing through some brush
the dog suddenly leaped upon him?

Stop scaring yourself! the boy told himself fiercely.
You've got to find Hero before Mr. Spinks does!

D.J. hurried on. A Steller's jay with a crested
topknot noisily scolded the boy for invading the forest's
silence. A gray squirrel ran across the brown pine
needles on the ground and leaped onto the trunk of a
sugar pine. Safely behind the trunk, the squirrel
chattered and called alarm signals. D.J. knew that if
Mr. Spinks was a woodsman, he'd come sneaking
up to see what was bothering the bird and animal.

D.J. was breathing hard and perspiration was
starting to form along his spine in spite of the sun

being blocked by the fast-moving clouds.

Near the summit of Lobo Mountain, with Saddleback Ridge in sight, D.J. stopped to rest at another small patch of dust. Probably birds had used it to dust their feathers because it was laced with bird tracks. D.J. carefully stepped over the spot and climbed on up the hill. In a few minutes, he circled carefuly around and came back.

Even before D.J. got within ten feet, he could clearly see the one lone dog track. The boy's blood surged through his body, getting him ready to run or defend himself. Fear dried the tongue in his mouth.

Now there was no doubt! D.J. was being followed by a dog he could not see; a dog that did not want to be seen.

As D.J. started to climb again, he suddenly froze. In a clearing where no trees grew on top of Saddleback Ridge, a shadow moved across wide areas of tumbled granite boulders.

"Mr. Spinks!" D.J. breathed. "He beat me to the pass!"

The boy was caught between the strange stalking dog behind and the armed man ahead! D.J. held his breath, watching.

At the summit of Lobo Mountain, Mr. Spinks stood at the start of Saddleback Ridge. He turned slowly, looking in all directions. He seemed to be making a choice. He took off his leather hat and tipped his face up to the threatening sky. Then he clapped his hat back on his head, adjusted the pistol at his belt, and started back down the hill the way he'd come.

He's giving up! D.J. thought. *He's quitting because of the storm getting so close!*

As soon as D.J. was sure Mr. Spinks couldn't hear him, he hurried toward the top and the level trail over Saddleback Ridge. D.J. still held his stick ready and kept his head twisting in all directions as he ran.

Even though the main danger had been removed, D.J. had to fight a terrible, rising urge to panic; to run from the unseen, unheard danger of the strange dog padding silently behind him in the forest. The back of D.J.'s neck seemed to have every short hair sticking straight up. His arms rippled with fear so that he could see the flesh crawl.

He didn't hear Hero barking anymore. D.J. struck the trail over Saddleback Ridge and started down the other side of Lobo Mountain. He began a steep climb off to the right, but he didn't recognize where he was until he rounded a stand of timber and saw the cattle guard and Mr. Schmekle's warning signs.

The cabin! It would be safe inside! The old recluse probably didn't have it locked. Most people in Stoney Ridge didn't lock their doors, and this shack was miles from anywhere.

D.J. eased his way carefully across the cattle guard so he wouldn't break an ankle. Once on the other side, the boy allowed himself a fast walk. He saw the brush pile and remembered the quail. When he passed the pile and several birds exploded in all directions, D.J. didn't even jump.

He turned to look behind him. There was no sign of the silent dog following him. Neither was there any sound of Hero's barking. D.J. spun back around and rapidly approached the cabin.

It was weathered and old, with one main room and a lean-to.* The sloping roof was supported against the back side of the shanty. Both had been made of logs and scrap lumber. There was no porch, but a large circle of Douglas fir had been laid down for a step. D.J. took one final look behind him before stopping in front of the door.

He started to turn back to the door when he saw a movement. Beyond the brush pile, a dog was just coming out of the brush by the side of the road. At first glance, D.J. thought it was Hero. Then the boy looked again and knew it wasn't.

The strange dog started trotting silently toward the cabin. D.J. turned and grabbed for the door handle.

He gave it a twist. It clicked open. Then the boy's hand froze on the knob. From inside came the unmistakable sound of a dog's toenails on a wooden floor. A low rumbling growl came through the door.

Swallowing hard, D.J. swiveled his head to look behind him. The strange dog was closing fast, coming silently but purposefully, straight for the boy. D.J. let go of the door handle and gripped the stick in both hands. Then he again turned toward the door. The toenail sound had stopped. The growl was deeper and closer, right behind the door.

While the boy stood in frightened uncertainty between the two dangers, the door swung slowly open!

Chapter Ten

A SURPRISE AT SADDLEBACK RIDGE

The cabin was dark inside, but D.J. saw the shape of a dog. As the boy swung his club up to defend himself, the dog barked once and leaped up, straight for D.J.!

The boy started to bring the club down hard when he recognized the bark. He stopped the strike and dropped the stick on the bare wooden floor. "HERO!"

The little hair-pulling bear dog's leap carried him into the boy's arms, knocking him off-balance. D.J. started to fall backward onto the ground. He automatically threw out his right hand and caught the doorjamb. D.J. spun halfway around, but he held onto his dog with his left arm.

Then D.J. saw the other dog. He was running hard, straight toward them across the cleared yard. Hero also saw the other dog and growled, struggling to be free, but D.J. held on tight and scrambled to regain his footing.

"No, Hero! No!"

The boy staggered forward into the shanty's dark interior. Instantly, D.J. kicked backward with his heavy boot. The door slammed shut.

A second later, the strange dog smashed into it so hard the door shuddered and seemed about to be knocked off its hinges. Hero barked like crazy and struggled so hard the boy couldn't hold him. The little mutt jumped to the bare wooden floor and threw himself at the closed door. A steady stream of the loudest barks D.J. had ever heard poured from the scroungy-looking little dog.

"'No, Hero! Quiet, I say!"

Reluctantly, the little mixed breed dog stopped barking. He growled deep in his throat for a moment, then slowly turned to look at the boy.

D.J. reached down suddenly and threw his arms around the dog. "Oh, Hero! I'm so glad to see you!"

The mutt was obviously glad to see the boy too. Hero licked D.J.'s face and seemed about to turn himself inside out with happiness.

For a minute, the boy and dog were close, the dog whining eagerly and happily; the boy whispering, "How did you get in here? Must've found the door open. Then the wind blew it shut after you got inside."

The door shuddered again. D.J. scrambled to his feet, his eyes scanning the cabin's interior for something to brace the door. He glimpsed a heavy wood box half filled with oak pieces waiting for burning in the old kitchen stove. The boy leaped to the box, tugged mightily, and heaved it against the door.

D.J. started to straighten up. The door shuddered

again as the outside dog crashed heavily into it. Hero threw himself at the door, barking furiously. It was then the boy realized not a sound had come from the strange dog outside. He didn't growl; he didn't bark. He assaulted the door in total, spooky silence! D.J.'s flesh crawled though he was now safely inside; or was he safe?

"Come on, Hero! Let's take a look around and be sure there's no other way that dog can get in here!"

There were two windows on either side of the tiny room. D.J. hurried to the closest one on the right, by the wood-burning stove. The pane hadn't been washed for years. Through the grime and spider webs, D.J. saw the ground outside slanted sharply away. The lowest part of the window was at least six feet off the ground. A big dog might have leaped that high, but the boy didn't think Hero could have done it, and the dog outside was almost exactly Hero's size.

D.J. checked the second window and found it was about the same as the first. Through it, the boy could see the sky was darker now. The evergreens stood motionless in a lull before the storm.

"I don't think that strange dog can make it through those windows, Hero. Hm? No other door in here, but what's in the lean-to?"

D.J. and his dog moved across the cluttered room, past a rickety pine table, past an old blasting powder box used for a chair, past a clutter of musty-smelling magazines and newspapers. D.J.'s eyes had adjusted to the semi-darkness enough so he could see there was a slight step downward into the lean-to.

No window. The boy's eyes determined that in a single quick glance. How about a door? The boy stepped cautiously down into the lean-to, his nose bringing the smell of unwashed bedding and dusty quilts. D.J. saw the bed in the corner. It was more of a cot, really, he decided. It was rumpled and untidy as though it had never been made.

But something moved on it!

D.J.'s reflexes caused his hands to jerk up into a defensive position and his legs to brace in a slight crouch. The boy's heart leaped into double-time speed.

But Hero didn't whine or growl. As the boy stood ready to defend himself, the dog trotted by him and up to the cot. Hero raised his front paws, placed them on the edge of the bed, and extended his muzzle. Hero whined softly.

"No, Hero! Down!" The boy's sharp command was instinctive.

The dog obeyed. D.J. moved slowly forward, straining to see what had moved on the cot.

Slowly, the boy saw what it was.

"Roger!"

D.J.'s whispered exclamation was followed by action. He leaned over the bed. His hand touched the little boy's naked chest.

"He's breathing!" D.J. cried. "Hero, he's alive!"

D.J. gently shook the tiny shoulders. "Roger! Roger! Wake up! Wake up!"

There was no response. D.J. started to shake the boy harder, then stopped.

He had never really seen any person who was unconscious, let alone in diabetic shock. But the mountain boy knew that's what he was looking at.

"Hero, what're we going to do?"

The dog whined and thrust his muzzle against D.J.'s pants leg. The boy stooped and gave him a quick, absent-minded pat. D.J.'s thoughts spun so fast he couldn't separate them for a moment. Then he forced himself to take a deep breath and think clearly.

"Hero, Roger will die if we don't get help soon! But how?"

D.J. hurriedly glanced around the lean-to. No phone. No C.B. radio; no shortwave or ham* outfit as some people who lived alone in the mountains had. D.J. stepped back into the small main room. Again, no phone or radio.

Hero whined anxiously, disturbed by D.J.'s sudden, excited movements. The boy reach down quickly and petted the dog's head.

"I don't know how to help that little kid, Hero! I can't call for help, and I can't go outside and run back to camp because of that dog out there."

That reminded D.J. He hadn't heard the strange animal trying to get in since the last time he'd slammed his body against the door. The boy moved to the window on his right and looked out.

The sky was darker. Thunder crashed closer. It echoed though the canyons and bounced off the granite walls and domes.

D.J. crossed to the other window and saw more of the same threatening sky and acres of evergreen trees.

The boy turned toward the door. He debated. Open it a crack and try to locate the dog? Well, even if the animal was out of sight, it didn't mean D.J. could dash out and down the mountain to the camp without getting attacked.

"But I can't just do nothing!" D.J. said fiercely,

looking down at Hero. "I've go to do *something*—
and fast! But what?"

D.J. moved to the door. He scooted the wood box
back half an inch. Slowly, the boy took hold of the
knob and eased the door open a crack. He put his
right eye to the opening and looked around the
yard.

*Old shed. Empty except for pieces of wire and
junk. Nothing big enough to hide the strange dog. Old
tankhouse is coming apart so I can look right
through the boards. No dog there.*

D.J.'s eye flickered on. *The woodpile? Yes, the dog
could be hiding behind that. Or maybe even that great
pile of dry brush farther out. Or maybe—what was
that?*

The boy adjusted his forehead against the crack in
the door so he could see better. He'd never seen
anything quite like that, whatever it was. It was
about five feet long, two feet wide, and three feet high.
It was like a wire box made of heavy gauge mesh
wire and metal frames instead of two-by-fours.

Then D.J. knew! He turned to Hero. "That's got to
be one of those humane traps Mr. Waymond told me
about!"

The boy again put his eye to the crack in the door.
The trap's spring-loaded door stood over the only
opening. If the strange dog would go in for the bait
and step on the trigger, the door would drop down and
catch him. D.J. could then run down the mountain
and get help.

The strange dog trotted silently into D.J.'s view.
The dog had been behind the brush pile. He passed it
going away toward the southeast stand of timber. In

a moment, the dog had disappeared into the brush
200 yards away.

D.J. closed the door and bent to pet his dog. "That
must be Mr. Schmekle's dog and the one that bit Roger.
But I don't know if the dog's given up and is going
off someplace, maybe miles away, or if he's just
waiting for us to step outside."

Hero whined and licked D.J.'s face. Absently, the
boy stood up and looked toward the lean-to.

"There has to be some way I can signal for help,
Hero! But how?"

The anguished words were barely out of his
mouth when D.J. remembered something Brother Paul
Stagg had preached about the Sunday before.

"There'll come a time in everyone's life," the giant
lay preacher had rumbled, "when there's nobody out
there but you and God. At first, a believer may feel
he's totally helpless and alone.

"But when he remembers the Lord is with him,
and he asks in faith—well, brothers and sisters—I tell
you for sure, that's when you can see the power of
God!"

D.J. groaned. Those were mighty good words to
hear in church, but out here in a cabin like this they
didn't seem to really be true. But what else could
D.J. do? When he'd been in the little church the other
night, he hadn't even been able to say a word. But he
had left there with a feeling that everything was going
to be all right.

What was it some famous Christian once said?
D.J. thought. *Never doubt in the dark what God has
shown you in the light.*

Right now, it didn't seem possible that even God

could help. But D.J. closed his eyes and softly prayed, "Please, Lord, show me what I can do!"

That was all, but the boy meant it sincerely. He opened his eyes. For the first time, he noticed a kerosene lamp and a box of kitchen matches on the rickety old table.

As D.J. reached out to remove the lamp's glass chimney, a thought hit him. He hesitated, thinking fast. Of course—a signal! But it was a terribly dangerous idea! It could get D.J. in awful trouble. Yet if he didn't do it, little Roger would surely die.

D.J. decided. He pulled the wood box away from the door and opened it. He took a quick look to be sure Mr. Schmekle's dog wasn't in sight. D.J. returned to the table, removed the lamp's chimney, then grabbed up the lamp base and the box of matches.

"Stay, Hero! Stay!" D.J. commanded. Then he opened the door and ran outside carrying the lamp in one hand and the box of matches in the other.

"Please, Lord! Let it work! Let it work!"

Chapter Eleven

DISASTER IN THE MOUNTAINS

D.J. bent low and ran hard toward the brush pile, his eyes searching the area where the strange dog had disappeared. The boy knew he was about to do a very dangerous thing with the lamp, something he would never do under ordinary circumstances. But he wasn't doing it for himself.

What else can I do? he thought desperately, running hard on his toes to lessen the sound of his boots. *That little boy will die if I don't get help fast, and this is the only way I can think of to do it.*

His thoughts snapped off as he saw the strange dog. The animal had been watching him, for it appeared suddenly at the edge of the undergrowth well beyond the brush pile at the southeast corner of the clearing.

D.J. slid to a stop, his heart trying to jump through his open mouth. His breath came in ragged sounds, partly from the exertion of running and partly from fear. The boy's skin crawled with goosebumps as he stood uncertainly for a minute. His eyes didn't leave the dog, but D.J.'s mind flickered down to the lamp and the matches.

Too far away to throw and be sure of hitting the brush pile. Besides, how would I light it? Better get out of here!

D.J. backed slowly toward the shack, watching the strange dog. It still stood at the edge of the clearing, just inside the line of brush and trees. But the dog's manner was menacing, with its head down and ears laid down flat against his skull.

Any minute, D.J. thought, *he'll charge me! But if I can get closer to the door, maybe I'll have a chance.*

The boy backed up steadily, wishing he'd thought to find a weapon. All he had was the lamp with its clear glass reservoir of kerosene. That would never stop the strange dog. If the dog moved toward him, D.J. knew he could only run as hard as he could toward the shanty door.

D.J. was within twenty feet of the cabin door before the watching dog moved. Silently, with his head down, the dog ran toward the boy. D.J. turned and dashed madly toward the cabin.

He shifted the lamp to his left hand with the matches and desperately twisted the doorknob. As the door opened, D.J. leaped inside and slammed the door shut with his heel. He set the lamp and matches down on the floor and used both hands to jerk the wood box against the door. Then D.J. collapsed against it, his heart thumping so hard he could feel the blood pounding in his ears.

A moment later, the strange dog hit the other side

of the door. Hero launched himself in defense, barking shrilly and trying to get at the silent dog.

D.J. ordered, "No, Hero! It's OK! Down!" The boy slid weakly down the door until his weight was on the wood box.

"Oh, Hero!" D.J. moaned, throwing his arms around the scroungy little mutt. "It's really all my fault! I've tried to make up for it, but nothing is working out right!"

The little dog licked D.J.'s face and whined anxiously, his stub tail vibrating from side to side as he tried to comfort the boy. But D.J. was too desperate and scared to be comforted.

When the strange dog didn't hurl himself at the door a second time, D.J. got up and walked to the window. The dog wasn't in sight. The boy crossed the deepening shadows of the tiny room to the other window. Nothing. D.J. turned back to the door.

He placed his ear against it and listened. Not a sound came from outside. He moved the wood box slightly with his boot and eased the door open a crack.

The strange dog was cautiously approaching the trap set by the animal control officer. "Please!" D.J. breathed, "let him go in! Let him get caught!"

The dog circled suspiciously, as a wild animal might have. The dog moved slowly around, his nose testing the air. He advanced cautiously toward the closed end of the trap, away from the open door.

"He smells the bait there," D.J. told Hero softly without taking his eyes from the crack in the door. "He's getting closer. Now he's sniffing through the wire. He's reaching his nose out. Can't get the food through the wire, though. If he'd just go around to the door and go in so that . . . he's giving up."

D.J. closed the shanty door and sat down on the wood box. He again started to hug Hero. Then D.J.'s head jerked up as he remembered something.

What was it the vet said about a rabid animal could be dying of thirst and hunger, but can't eat if he can't close his jaws? But this dog's lower jaw isn't hanging loose, so that must mean he's not in the advanced stages yet. He's not paralyzed, so he could eat! But he's confused or scared, so he won't go in that trap.

The boy returned to the door and peeked out. The dog was again circling around the trap, but not going near the open end with the door standing high above it, ready to fall when the trigger was tripped.

"Maybe he doesn't like the dog food Mr. Waymond used for bait," D.J. told Hero. "Hey!" The boy spun around. "Maybe Mr. Schmekle had some special food for his dog. I'll bet you're starved, Hero! No telling how long you've been locked in here. I don't suppose it'll be wrong to use some of that dog food for you, huh? Let's see what we can find."

D.J. shoved the wood box into place against the door and rapidly searched the cupboard by the wood-burning stove. His eyes skimmed past the canned goods, a sack of dry red beans, and some pasta. The boy bent over and jerked open a small door under the cupboard.

"Here it is, Hero! A whole bag full of dry dog food! You get some first, and then I'll see if I can fix up that strange dog with something too."

The boy found a pot and a little water in a pail by

the door. "You thirsty, Hero? There's not much water left, and there's no faucet in here. Tell you what. I'll mix the dog food first and then you can drink what water is left. OK?"

The little hair-puller whined and wiggled his stub tail as D.J. poured the dog food into the pot and added the liquid. "There's not much water, Hero, so it's going to be pretty dry. But maybe there's enough so it will do."

D.J. heard the thunder growing ominously louder as the storm approached from the southeast. Through the grimy window on that side, the boy could see the tall stately evergreens at the edge of the clearing. They were silent and still.

The boy scooped out a double handful of the dog food and dropped it on the table top. He bent and placed the pot with the remaining food on the floor. "Here, try this."

Hero sniffed the semi-dry mixture and took a mouthful. Then he gulped it ravenously.

As D.J. watched, an idea popped into his mind. Immediately, he stood and began kneading the mixture he'd left on the table. He then rolled globs of the dog food in his hands, as if he were making a snowball. He held up the first one and looked at it.

Should hold together in the air, he told himself. *Let's see how many more I can make.*

When he had made several small balls of the semi-moist mixture, D.J. wiped his hands on an old flour sack and looked down with satisfaction.

"Well, guess that's it, Hero. Let's see if my idea works."

Hero finished eating and whined for more, but the

boy ignored him. D.J. moved to the door. Through the crack, he could see the strange dog. He was lying down some distance from the trap, looking at it.

"He's really hungry, I guess, but he's suspicious too. Well, Hero, here goes," D.J. said. He slowly slid the door open and stepped outside with half a dozen of the dog-food balls.

The strange dog's head swung toward the boy. The dog did not rise; he just watched as D.J. took two steps from the door. He raised his right hand and threw the first ball. It went wide to the right.

Too nervous! D.J. told himself fiercely. *Got to get hold of myself! Try again.*

The second ball went fairly straight, landing short of the trap. The dog did not move; his eyes stayed on D.J. He threw the third ball.

"Ah! Good!" He told himself aloud. "Right outside the trap door! But that ol' dog's not moving! Maybe if I can put one right by him. . . . "

D.J. took another step away from the shanty, leaned well back, and threw a ball as hard as he could. Pieces flew off in the air, but the main part struck the strange dog in the shoulder.

The boy leaped for the door and stepped inside, ready to slam the door. But the strange dog did not chase him. Instead, he picked up the dog-food ball that had hit him. He swallowed it and moved toward the other balls. In a moment, he stood outside the trap door, swallowing the last ball.

"Don't stop now!" D.J. whispered. "Go inside and see what kind of food's in there!"

For a moment, the strange dog hesitated. Then he stuck his nose inside the open end of the trap. He sniffed so loudly D.J. could hear him.

"Just one more step!" D.J. whispered. "Just one more—there! He did it!"

The strange dog stepped on the trigger. The spring-loaded door dropped hard, hitting the dog on his short tail. He leaped forward, then tried to turn. But it was too late.

"He's caught!" D.J. yelled, pulling open the door. "He's caught!"

The strange dog was no longer silent. He seemed to roar with rage as he tore at the strong steel mesh. For a moment, D.J. thought the dog was going to bite right through the wire.

"Maybe he will tear up that trap, Hero," D.J. said, turning around, "but not before I can do something."

The boy's mind twisted and turned with possibilities. *Run to the camp and get help? Will Roger live long enough for me to do that? If I get caught in that storm, lightning can hit me! That dog'll maybe get out of the trap if I wait."*

It was D.J.'s choice, and his alone. Whatever he did was his responsibility, and there would be a severe penalty, no matter what he did. But as he turned to look into the soft darkness of the lean-to where Roger Spinks lay dying in a diabetic coma, D.J. made his decision.

He ordered, "Stay! Hero! Stay!" D.J. again grabbed up the lamp and the matches. He opened the door and sprinted toward the brush pile.

He stopped, hurriedly unscrewed the lamp's wick and dropped it on the ground. He poured kerosene from the lamp onto the nearest part of the brush, leaving a three-foot trail of liquid in the dry grass as a fuse. D.J. lit one match and touched it to the kerosene trail. Instantly, small yellow flames leaped up.

The boy jumped back as the fire reached the edge of the brushpile where he'd poured the kerosene. As the dry clippings began to snap and crackle, the boy opened the match box and threw it into the flames.

Whoosh!

In an instant, bright yellow fire leaped into the air, sending columns of brown and gray smoke toward the sky.

D.J. backed up in surprise. It was a *lot* more fire than he had imagined. "Maybe I shouldn't have done it!" he whispered as the fire boiled higher and higher.

But there was no way of stopping it now!

D.J. lifted his eyes toward Lobo Peak Fire Lookout Station. He could not see the tower where the couple kept watch, but he knew they should see the smoke.

"Please!" the boy whispered. "See it now!"

D.J. knew what happened when fire lookouts spotted smoke or flame. They pinpointed it with equipment and radioed in the exact location. In minutes, the air commander from the California Forestry Service would be overhead in his plane to evaluate the situation.

D.J. figured they would see him in the clearing, frantically waving to them. They'd radio for the aerial tankers to fly over and drop fire retardant chemicals on the flames. The air commander would also call in a helicopter.

D.J. would carry the unconscious boy outside where the chopper could pick him up and fly him directly to a hospital. D.J. hoped it wouldn't be too late for Roger.

D.J.'s thoughts were interrupted by a soft sighing sound. He glanced up just as the tops of the southeast stand of evergreen trees bent from the first gust of wind from the advancing storm.

"The wind's coming up!" D.J. cried. "Oh, no! Not now!"

The first gust passed the trees and kicked up a dust devil at the southeastern edge of the cleared area. The small cyclone-like mass of whirling dust and debris raced downwind across the open space toward the trees on the northwest side.

A second gust of wind hit the boy's face. He felt his hair blown back around his ears. D.J. frantically turned back to the brush pile. It was roaring loudly and turning bright as the rising wind whipped through the dry branches and grass.

Desperately, D.J. looked around for a way to put out the fire.

But now the gusts were settling down to a steady blow that made tree tops moan and the brush pile flare up higher. The rising wind sucked up burning embers that sailed up into the air and over D.J.'s head.

As some landed on the open ground behind him, the boy was already running toward them. He stamped them out with his boots. But as the embers dissolved into smoke, the wind rose to a steady shriek.

More embers sailed into the air, moving higher and faster than the first ones. They landed farther away, near the northwest stand of trees.

Frantically, D.J. dashed toward the scattered hot spots and again stamped frantically. In a moment, they were all out. D.J. started to sigh with relief.

Then he glanced toward the cabin and his heart nearly stopped.

Burning embers from the brush pile had fallen on the dry pine needles on the roof.

The cabin was on fire with Hero and Roger inside!

Chapter Twelve

HELP FROM ON HIGH

D.J. had never run so fast in his life. In seconds, he was across the yard and through the cabin door. Hero leaped up to greet him.

"Out!" D.J. commanded, pointing through the open door. "Outside! NOW!"

Surprised at the sharpness in D.J.'s tone, the hair-puller lowered his ears, tucked his stub tail tight against his body, and scooted out the door.

The boy raced across the room and leaped down into the lean-to. In one quick movement he bent over Roger and shook his bare shoulders.

"Roger! Wake up! Roger?"

The little boy's head rolled loosely in D.J.'s grip. He picked up the unconscious boy, but Roger's 60 pounds of weight made D.J. stagger. D.J. almost tripped stepping up into the main cabin and Roger's loosely dangling arms caught on the door. Still, D.J. managed to stumble across the floor and out the door.

There D.J. was forced to ease his burden down in the dirt for a moment. But D.J. could smell the smoke from the burning roof. He thought he could hear the fire snapping and crackling, but his own desperate breathing made it hard to be sure. He was looking at the fire on the roof when flames suddenly shot straight out from the attic.

"Lord, help!" D.J. cried, hooking his hands under Roger's armpits. Desperately, D.J. tugged, stepping backward. The unconscious boy's body slid across the open ground, his bare heels dragging in the dust.

Hero got excited at the unusual commotion. He ran back to D.J. and began barking and jumping toward Roger's torn and dirty cutoffs.

"No, Hero! Down!" D.J.'s sharp voice again drove the little dog back in uncertainty. The mountain boy didn't slow up. He backed rapidly away from the cabin as the whole place was quickly engulfed in bright yellow flames.

Rebuffed again, Hero turned his excitement against the other dog. Hero ran toward the trap, barking furiously. The strange dog bit viciously at his wire enclosure, trying to get out to answer Hero's challenge.

D.J. saw some of the heavy gauge mesh had been bent and a small opening made.

"No, Hero!" D.J. cried again, still dragging Roger's limp body well away from the burning shanty. "Come here!"

Again, the scroungy little mutt dropped his ears and tucked his stub tail, unsure why he couldn't do anything to please D.J. The boy barely noticed, for his eyes skittered around the disaster he had just created.

The brush pile was one long mound of intense fire. Yellow-red flames leaped twenty feet or more into the air. Most of the dense brownish-gray smoke rolled upward toward the overcast sky, but some smoke twisted across the yard, choking the boy. He coughed hard and finally stopped to rub his stinging eyes.

The cabin's roof began to buckle in the middle, breaking off small pieces of burning debris. It was sucked up by the wind and carried through the air toward the downwind trees and brush. If those caught fire, flames would roar through the whole forested mountainside.

"Oh, no!" D.J. moaned, lowering Roger's small body to the ground. "What have I done?"

He heard the approaching drone of a single plane even above the fire's roar. D.J. glanced upward, checking the sky. He turned rapidly in his tracks until he saw a tiny speck.

"There!" He pointed across the tree tops downwind from the brush pile. "The air commander! He's come to check out the smoke! See him, Hero?"

D.J. dragged Roger's limp body to a place that was fairly clear of smoke. D.J. lowered the little boy's shoulders to the ground. D.J. looked at the sky and jumped up and down. He waved frantically and shouted.

"Hey! We're over here! Down here!"

For a second, D.J. thought the plane was going to fly on without seeing them. He tried yelling and waving again, but his voice broke off as some smoke curled toward him and sent him into a coughing spasm.

It left him weak with his eyes burning, but D.J. looked up just as the light plane's orange-tipped wings wiggled. The aircraft went into a sharper bank and came back, wings tipping up and down in a signal of recognition.

"They've seen us!" D.J. cried, rubbing his smarting eyes and bending to pick up Roger's shoulders again. "Hero! They've seen us! They'll radio for help! It's going to be all right!"

D.J. glanced back at the unconscious boy. The ground smoke was getting much worse. D.J. told himself furiously, "I've got to get Roger farther away, out in the open so a helicopter can land! It can't land close to the fire! Hero, stay close!"

D.J. hooked his hands under Roger's armpits and stumbled backward, dragging Roger past the intense heat of the brush pile, moving into the wind. D.J. coughed hard and wiped his eyes on his shoulders, but he did not stop or let go of Roger.

It was hard going, but gradually D.J. pulled Roger farther away from the fire and close to the southeastern line of evergreens. Roger's bare heels made little trails in the dirt. Hero kept close to D.J.'s feet, sneezing at the dense smoke in his nose.

When D.J. reached the edge of the clearing, right against the trees, he stopped to cough and catch his breath. Through bleary, smarting eyes, the boy glanced up into the sky.

The wind died down suddenly though the sky was darker and more threatening. The air commander had climbed well above the fire, obviously waiting for the aerial tankers to arrive so they could be directed on their run and drop.

Suddenly, D.J. heard a heavier beat in the air. He spun around, searching the glowering sky until he located the helicopter. It was sleek and fast, skimming the treetops, sending their slender branches into wild spasms as the wind from the overhead blade rushed upon them.

"They're coming! Hero, they're coming!"

The mountain boy let out a wild yell and jumped up and down, waving his hands over his head. He cupped his hands and yelled again though he knew the people in the chopper couldn't hear him.

"Hurry! Please hurry!"

The aircraft swung upwind away from the fire and smoke. The whirlybird settled to the open ground fairly close to the southeastern stand of trees. That was some distance from where D.J. had left Roger stretched out on the earth.

The chopper's overhead blades stirred up dust in a wild storm. D.J. closed his eyes and spun away to protect his face, but not before he had recognized the blue and gold insignia of the California Highway Patrol.

The helicopter's engines changed sounds. D.J. turned slowly and carefully opened his eyes. A stocky technician leaped from the aircraft to the ground. He wore a short-sleeved summer CHP uniform with a gold helmet and visor. He pushed that up with his left hand and carried a jump bag in the other hand. He wore a flight vest of olive-drab with many pockets containing first-aid medications. The officer doubled over and ran toward D.J.

With Hero barking excitedly at his heels, the boy

dashed to meet the man.

"Boy!" D.J. cried, "I'm glad you're here!" He pointed. "Help that little kid! I can't wake him up!"

The stocky officer bent so his gold helmet glistened in front of D.J.'s eyes. "You OK?"

"Yeah! But Roger's not!"

The technician spoke quickly. "I've got to take his vital signs and get him stabilized while the pilot shuts down the aircraft. You stay here! Keep your dog with you unless the pilot tells you differently!" Then the officer ran toward Roger.

D.J. was almost trembling with fear and excitement as he listened to the helicopter's engines sink to a whisper. The overhead blade slowly stopped turning. The pilot stepped out of the plastic bubble and dashed toward D.J. The boy saw the pilot was about six feet tall. He also wore a full uniform with a helmet and a holstered gun.

He ran up to D.J. and Hero and stooped over to look into the boy's eyes. "What've we got, son?"

Quickly, D.J. explained. The pilot interrupted and stood up. "That's the lost kid? The one with diabetes?"

D.J. nodded and started to explain more, but the pilot interrupted. "You stay right here! I've got to tell the technician about the diabetic coma. That takes different emergency treatment than most cases! Then we've got to get out of here! That fire's too close and the storm's about to hit us."

The scruffy hair-puller whined and thrust his muzzle against D.J.'s pants leg. The boy bent and gave his dog a reassuring pat on the shoulder while the two officers worked over the still, small form of Roger Spinks.

D.J. groaned. "I hope he's going to be all right! But I'm in terrible trouble, Hero! Terrible, terrible trouble!"

The mutt licked the boy's hand as if to comfort D.J. "Oh," D.J. said, "I almost forgot! He tipped his head up to the sky. "Thanks, Lord! Thanks for bringing those men! And please—let them save Roger!"

The pilot soon ran back past D.J. and Hero. Without stopping, the officer called, "He's almost stabilized! I've got to get the longboard* for him! You stay put!"

D.J. nodded and watched as the pilot reached into the backseat area of the helicopter. In seconds, he sprinted back carrying something that looked like an ironing board with straps.

As he passed the boy and dog, the pilot called, "Follow me! You can help!"

"I'm coming," D.J. replied, leaping to his feet and snapping his fingers for Hero to follow.

When D.J. reached Roger, the technician had inserted a needle with a long plastic tube into the arm of the unconscious boy.

"Here," the technician said, turning to D.J. "Hold this I.V.* for me, please! Keep it up so the saline solution will run down. He's dehydrated!* That's common in diabetic cases."

D.J. lifted the clear, soft plastic bottle above his head, careful not to pull the tube too tightly and jerk the needle from Roger's arm. Hero seemed to think D.J. was holding up something to jump at, like a ball.

Hero started leaping up to reach it.

"No," the boy said with less firmness than earlier. "No, Hero! Down! That's a good dog!"

D.J. watched as the officers strapped Roger to the board. Then together they lifted him.

The technician said, "We're going to run to the chopper. You run with us! Stay close with that I.V."

The boy nodded. The two officers hurried toward the helicopter supporting the longboard with its still figure on it. D.J. stayed even with them while Hero trotted at their heels. The pilot called without looking around.

"When we get to the chopper, you get in the left front seat and strap yourself in. You understand?"

"My dog! What'll you do with my dog?"

"He'll have to ride in back on the floor with the technician and the little boy."

D.J. had never been that close to a helicopter. He handed the I.V. bag over to the pilot. Then D.J. ran around the front of the aircraft to the left side. He crawled into the bubble-like area with the pilot's instrument panel to the right. D.J. twisted to look behind him.

The men lifed the unconscious boy and placed his board on the gurney so it was crossways in the plane. The technician scrambled in after Roger, moving among the emergency equipment and settling into the rear seat.

"My dog!" D.J. cried.

"Don't worry!" the pilot called. He bent out of sight and stood up again with Hero in his arms. "Kid, make your dog lie down and stay still!"

D.J. nodded and spoke to his dog. Hero stretched

out beside the gurney and looked up at D.J. as the technician strapped himself in.

The pilot climbed into the right front seat beside D.J. "You buckled up tight, Son?"

D.J. could only nod. The pilot's hands moved rapidly, hitting switches and controls. The chopper's engines whined as they revved up.

"Here we go!" the pilot cried.

The sleek helicopter leaped into the air, giving D.J. a funny feeling in his stomach. He saw the trees drop away below as the chopper climbed rapidly toward the threatening gray skies.

The boy caught a glint of something off to his right. He quickly made out two fast-moving airplanes boring in toward the fire, well above the line of evergreen trees.

"Look!" the mountain boy cried, pointing.

"I see them!" the pilot answered. "Aerial tankers to put out the fire."

D.J. wanted to cheer as the first twin-engine airplane with its high tail dipped toward the fire. The plane flew low and leveled out. D.J. saw the lean-to collapse upon itself. The rest of the cabin was totally engulfed in flames. Then the first aerial tanker released a sheet of pink retardant. It cascaded prettily down on the shack and smothered the fire. It went out.

"Wow!" the boy cried, turning to the pilot. "Did you see that?"

D.J. didn't wait for an answer. He turned to look below at the scene rapidly falling behind.

Well out of the smoke and safe from the fiery brush pile, the strange dog was still struggling in the trap. D.J. saw it look up as the second plane dumped its load on the brush pile. The flames vanished.

The fires were out!

Then D.J. couldn't see any more. The helicopter banked sharply, climbing high above the trees. Then it leveled out and streaked away, racing the storm; racing to save a little unconscious boy's life.

D.J. could see the pilot's lips moving and guessed he was talking to the rear seat technician by radios in their helmets. However, a moment later D.J. heard the technician radio the hospital.

"Timbergold Memorial, this is Helicopter 12. We're inbound to your facility with an E.T.A.* of 10 minutes. We have a 7-year-old male about 30 kilograms* weight. Child is unconscious and unresponsive. We have a reported history of diabetes. We believe he hasn't had his insulin in the last 48 hours."

D.J. couldn't catch all the rest. Slowly, he sank against the safety belts and closed his eyes. "Please!" he whispered. "Let Roger be all right!"

He didn't open his eyes until he felt the helicopter settle upon the helipad* at the hospital. D.J. saw the emergency team rushing toward the chopper.

The pilot's hand moved rapidly as he shut down the engines. He grinned at D.J.

"Well, we beat the storm and the little kid's still alive. We've done all we can! Let's hope it's enough!"

Chapter Thirteen

D.J. AND THE LAW

Two days later, D.J. answered a knock at the front door. Everyone had gone to town, but D.J. had to finish writing his story for the newspaper, so he was home alone.

D.J.'s heart nearly stopped at the sight of Mr. Spinks. The boy's eyes darted to the bearded man's belt. There was no weapon, but he reached out a tattooed forearm and opened the screen door. The boy backed up, but Mr. Spinks grabbed D.J.'s right hand.

"Kid, I would have hurt you bad if I could've caught you out there on Lobo Mountain. I would've killed your dog and later beat up on your father too. But my boy. . . . " Mr. Spinks' voice nearly broke before he finished. "My son's alive because of what you did. And because of your little dog too. So I come to apologize."

D.J. didn't hear much more. He was so weak

117

when Mr. Spinks left that he sank into a big chair
and shook with relief.

* * * * *

The next evening, D.J. sat on the edge of the same
big chair and looked at Corporal Brackett. The boy
swallowed hard, expecting that the deputy had
come to arrest him for starting the fire.

The Dillon family had gathered around D.J. Dad
and Two Mom were standing behind him on the left
and Grandpa Dillon stood on the right. The old
man's thin fingers patted the boy's shoulder
reassuringly as the deputy took out his notepad and
a pen.

Corporal Brackett sat down in a straight-back
chair borrowed from the dining room and leaned
forward to look straight into D.J.'s face. The boy
shifted his gaze behind the officer to where Alfred sat
on a synthetic leather couch with Pris, Kathy, and
Mrs. Stagg. Brother Paul Stagg stood beside Corporal
Brackett as he cleared his throat and began.

"You understand, D.J., that you did a terrible
thing in starting that fire?"

D.J. nodded, looking at the floor where Hero slept
with his muzzle across the boy's boot.

"You broke the law," Corporal Brackett continued. "You risked destroying thousands of acres of
prime timber and loss of lives."

"I know," D.J.'s voice was barely a whisper.

Grandpa said, "Now, hold just a dadburned
minute there, Mr. Law Officer! My grandson. . . . "

Brother Paul broke in. "Excuse me, Mr. Dillon,
sir—but I believe this here deputy has a right to have
his say. But I hope, Corporal Brackett, you'll

remember that Scripture says in First John 1:9, 'If we confess our sins, He is faithful and just to forgive us our sins, and to cleanse us from all unrighteousness.' This boy has confessed his sins before God, because he already told me he had. Now he's confessing before men."

The deputy looked at the lay preacher and said, "God's in the forgiving business, but the law is interested in enforcement and justice. My job is to file a follow-up report on this case."

"I'm sorry," Brother Paul said gently. "Go ahead."

The deputy turned back to the boy. "D.J., you took upon yourself the reponsibility to risk the lives of all those people. I don't just mean the CHP officers and aerial tanker pilots, but the tanker crews that drove in to do the mop-up. You risked the life of that little boy plus your own."

D.J. raised his head slightly. "I realized that it was dangerous to start a fire out there! If it were just Hero and me, I wouldn't have done it! But that was the only way I could think of to keep Roger from dying! I'm responsible—so do whatever you have to do to me!"

Dad gripped D.J.'s left shoulder hard and shifted his weight as though he were going to come out with fighting words. But the deputy held up his hand and Dad didn't say anything. The officer looked at D.J.

"I see," he said solemnly.

Deputy Brackett stood up slowly and faced the others. "This young man was alone, facing a terrible choice that even an adult wouldn't relish. He had to decide whether to do nothing and let the diabetic boy die, or set that fire and take a chance somebody would see the smoke and send help in time to save the boy and put out the fire."

D.J. raised his eyes, unsure of what the officer was saying.

Corporal Brackett continued quietly, "You took upon yourself the responsibility to save someone else's life without regard for the consequences of what could happen to you, then or later. Because of that, Roger Spinks is going to live. The scent dog wouldn't have gotten there in time. The storm would have ruined any trail. Of course, it's too bad Roger's having to have those shots because the lab report showed that Schmekle's dog was rabid. But those injections are rather painless now. So it's all turned out all right."

D.J. glanced at his family. They were all listening hard to the deputy. He continued.

"Incidentally, the coroner found the old man apparently suffered a heart attack after his dog turned on him."

The deputy paused and looked through the Dillons' front-room window where Hero was tied.

"D.J., the hospital told me that, as cold as it was at night in the open mountains, the little boy could easily have developed a hypothermal condition* and died of exposure. But Roger told them that your dog found him and kept him warm the first night by sleeping close to him."

Grandpa cackled like a Rhode Island red hen and pounded his rubber-tipped Irish shillelagh on the floor. "Them was three dog nights,* but one dog's a powerful amount of heat when you're just a little shaver like that lost boy!"

Corporal Brackett didn't seem to notice the interruption. "A bear or something came near in the night, but Hero chased it off. The next morning, they stumbled upon the cabin. The boy said he was so tired he just fell on the bed. That's all he remembers until he woke up in the hospital. But we know the rest."

Corporal Brackett closed his notebook with a snap. "I'll send my report through channels, of course, but I'm going to point out the extenuating circumstances.* D.J., you took the responsibility to save someone else's life without regard for your own safety. I'll point out that only a boy of personal integrity would have accepted that kind of responsibility. I doubt there'll be any severe punishment for you. But don't let it happen again!"

D.J. blinked fast, remembering the good feeling he'd had in the church: it would turn out all right. "I won't!" he promised fervently.

The deputy said, "One thing more, D.J. See that your dog gets his rabies vaccination and a license!"

"I've already done that! See Hero's new collar and license tags?"

The officer bent to check and straightened up to smile at everyone. "So he has! Well, guess that's about it for now. Goodnight, all."

When the officer walked down the front steps, everyone crowded around D.J., laughing and shaking his hand or hugging him or pounding him on the back and shoulders.

Brother Paul Stagg's deep bass voice rumbled up from his giant chest. "The good Lord was with D.J. and you all through this trouble! Reckon we should all join hands and say thanks, don't you?"

With everyone in a circle, holding hands, D.J. bowed his head and murmured, "Thanks again, Lord! Just as soon as this prayer's finished, I'm going to start teaching Hero to always come when I call!"

"Amen," Brother Paul said.

D.J. wasn't sure if it was to end the prayer or to echo his thoughts. Either way, it was a good feeling.

D.J. raised his eyes and grinned happily at everyone. They smiled back. D.J. hoped the good feeling would last a long, long time.

And it did—until D.J.'s next exciting adventure. Read about it in the next book of the D.J. Dillon Adventure Series:

The Legend of the White Raccoon

LIFE IN STONEY RIDGE

BATON: A long club carried by law enforcement officers.

CHEVRON: A badge that has stripes which meet at an angle. A chevron is worn on the sleeve to show an officer's rank. A corporal has two such stripes.

CHOKE-SETTER: A lumberman who prepares downed trees for the heavy equipment that will take the trees out of the woods. The choke-setter digs a hole or tunnel under the downed tree trunk. Then he throws a strong steel cable over the log and pulls it back through the hole. He puts the knob on one end of the cable through a loop on the other end and pulls the cable tight around the log. A tread-type tractor then hooks onto the log and pulls it out of the woods.

CONIFERS: Another name for the many cone-bearing evergreen trees or shrubs. Spruce, fir, and pine trees are all conifers.

DEHYDRATED: The loss of water or moisture from the human body.

DIABETES: A disease that impairs the body's ability to use sugar.

DICKER: To bargain.

DOUBLE-OUGHT BUCKSHOT: Large pellets from a shotgun.

DUNGAREES: Blue denim work clothes, such as overalls or jeans.

E.T.A.: An abbreviation for "estimated time of arrival."

EXTENUATING CIRCUMSTANCES: Forgivable difficulties that make a wrongdoing seem less serious.

FOXTAIL: Grass that has a "head" with a sharp, arrow-like point. A foxtail may enter a dog's body and keep moving deeper, causing infection, since the foxtail often cannot be pulled back out.

GET CRACKIN': Another way of saying "get moving fast."

HAIR-PULLING BEAR DOG: A small, quick dog of mixed breed. A hair-puller's natural tendency is to go for the heels or backside of any animal, including sheep, cows, or bears.

HAM: An amateur radio operator licensed by the Federal Communications Commission. A ham operator usually broadcasts from equipment located in his home.

HELIPAD: An area that helicopters use for taking off and landing.

HIPPIES: Young people of the late 1960s who rejected society's values and wore unusual clothes.

HYDROPHOBIA: Another name for rabies. Hydrophobia originally meant "fear of water." It was once mistakenly believed that rabid (or "mad") animals were afraid of water.

HYPOTHERMAL CONDITION: A medical term used to describe a person with a subnormal temperature.

INSULIN: A substance used in the treatment of diabetes.

IRISH SHILLELAGH (pronounced "Shuh-**LAY**-Lee"): A cudgel or short, thick stick often used for a walking cane. A shillelagh is usually made of blackthorn saplings or oak and is named after the Irish village of Shillelagh.

I.V.: Intravenous; a medical fluid from a bottle and tube which is injected into a sick or injured person. The I.V. liquid slowly flows into the sick person's bloodstream.

KILOGRAMS: A metric measure of weight; a kilogram equals approximately 2.2 pounds.

LEAN-TO: A shed or similar building with a single pitch roof where the high end joins a taller building.

LIGHT TABLE: A table with a frosted glass top. Lights underneath the glass shine through paper or other materials placed on top of the glass. A light table is often used for pasting together the stories and pictures of a newspaper before it is printed.

LONGBOARD: A long, narrow board used by paramedics to move an injured person.

MOUNTAIN MISERY: A low-growing, fernlike mountain plant that gives off a bad smell when it is touched or walked upon. The plant is full of resin which explodes in a fire. Because of this, forestry people usually burn it to keep it under control. Mountain misery, also called "bear clover," has a pretty white flower which looks like snow. *Kitkit dizze* is the Indian name for mountain misery.

OL' NICK: A folk name for the devil.

PALAVERING: Idle talk or chatter.

PONDEROSA PINES: Large North American trees used for lumber. Ponderosa pines usually grow in the mountain regions of the West and can reach heights of 200 feet. The ponderosa pine is the state tree of Montana.

PUFF: Another name for newspaper stories that are sent in for publication but aren't really "news." A "puff" story puffs up the person the story is written about. It usually makes the subject of the story sound too good to be true.

SIDEBAR: A shorter, related news story placed next to a major story on the same subject.

STRINGER: A newspaper reporter who sometimes writes for a publication. A stringer is not a member of a newspaper's regular staff of reporters.

THREE DOG NIGHTS: A hound dog hunter's way of saying that it was so cold he would have to sleep with three dogs around him to keep warm.

D.J. DILLON

• ADVENTURE SERIES •

The Hair-Pulling Bear Dog
D.J.'s ugly mutt gets a chance to prove his courage.

The City Bear's Adventures
When his pet bear causes trouble in Stoney Ridge, D.J. realizes he can't keep the cub forever.

Dooger, The Grasshopper Hound
D.J. and his buddy Alfred rely on an untrained hound to save Alfred's little brother from a forest fire.

The Ghost Dog of Stoney Ridge
D.J. and Alfred find out what's polluting the mountain lakes—and end up solving the ghost dog mystery.

Mad Dog of Lobo Mountain
D.J. struggles to save his dog's life and learns a hard lesson about responsibility.

The Legend of the White Raccoon
Is the white raccoon real or only a phantom? As D.J. tries to find out, he stumbles upon a dangerous secret.

The Mystery of the Black Hole Mine
D.J. battles "gold" fever, and learns an eye-opening lesson about his own selfishness and greed.

Ghost of the Moaning Mansion
Will D.J. and Alfred get scared away from the moaning mansion before they find the "real" ghost?

THE EXITORN ADVENTURES

Got an appetite for fantasy, adventure, and humor? Then turn to these imaginative Christian novels, set in the make-believe kingdom of Exitorn. Here you'll meet 12-year-old Brill and his daredevil friend, Segra. Their stories, full of fast-paced action and suspense, will keep you turning the pages to see what will happen next.

Brill and the Dragators

Brill longs for his humble farm home when he is brought to the palace as a companion to the crown prince of Exitorn. The emperor and his son live only for pleasure and Brill remembers how different they are from his grandfather who lives for God. Will Brill and Segra be able to help the former king escape from prison and overthrow the evil emperor? (6-1344)

Segra and Stargull

In this second book of the Exitorn Adventures, Segra and Brill journey through Exitorn, across stormy seas, and into a neighboring country seeking Segra's parents. Their adventures call for courage and faith as time and again Segra risks her life and Brill's to help someone in need. Will Brill and Segra find her missing parents? Will Segra's bravery require the ultimate test of courage for her and Brill? (6-1345)

Dear Reader:

We would like to know your thoughts about the book you've just read. Your ideas will help us as we seek to publish books that will interest you.

Send your responses to: **Winner Books
1825 College Avenue
Wheaton, IL 60187**

What made you decide to read Mad Dog of Lobo Mountain?

- ☐ I bought it for myself.
- ☐ My parents bought it for me.
- ☐ It was a gift.
- ☐ It was part of a school assignment.
- ☐ It was loaned to me by a friend.

What did you like most about this book? (You can check more than one answer.)

- ☐ Characters
- ☐ Humor
- ☐ Animals
- ☐ Adventure
- ☐ Mystery
- ☐ Glossary
- ☐ Story
- ☐ Inside art sketches
- ☐ Romance
- ☐ Other: _____

From the following list, please check the subjects you would like to read about in the future. (You can check more than one answer.)

- ☐ Sports
- ☐ Make-believe
- ☐ Science fiction
- ☐ History
- ☐ Scary stories
- ☐ Mysteries
- ☐ Comics
- ☐ Other: _____
- ☐ Animals
- ☐ Devotional books
- ☐ Real people

Would you be interested in reading other Winner books? (Check only one answer.)

- ☐ Very interested
- ☐ A little bit interested
- ☐ Not at all interested

How old are you? _____

Would you be interested in a Winner book club? If so, please fill in your name and address below:

NAME: _____

ADDRESS: _____

_____

Winner Books are produced by Victor Books and are designed to entertain and instruct young readers in Christian principles.

Other Winner Books you will enjoy:

The Mystery Man of Horseshoe Bend by Linda Boorman
The Drugstore Bandit of Horseshoe Bend by Linda Boorman
The Hairy Brown Angel and Other Animal Tails edited by Grace Fox Anderson
The Peanut Butter Hamster and Other Animal Tails edited by Grace Fox Anderson
Skunk for Rent and Other Animal Tails edited by Grace Fox Anderson
The Incompetent Cat and Other Animal Tails edited by Grace Fox Anderson
The Duck Who Had Goosebumps and Other Animals Tails edited by Grace Fox Anderson
The Pint-Sized Piglet and Other Animal Tails edited by Grace Fox Anderson
The Mysterious Prowler by Frances Carfi Matranga
The Forgotten Treasure by Frances Carfi Matranga
The Mystery of the Missing Will by Frances Carfi Matranga
The Big Top Mystery by Frances Carfi Matranga
The Hair-Pulling Bear Dog by Lee Roddy
The City Bear's Adventures by Lee Roddy
Dooger, the Grasshopper Hound by Lee Roddy
The Ghost Dog of Stoney Ridge by Lee Roddy
Mad Dog of Lobo Mountain by Lee Roddy
The Legend of the White Raccoon by Lee Roddy
The Mystery of the Black Hole Mine by Lee Roddy
Ghost of the Moaning Mansion by Lee Roddy
The Boyhood of Ranald Bannerman by George MacDonald
The Genius of Willie MacMichael by George MacDonald
The Wanderings of Clare Skymer by George MacDonald
Brill and the Dragators by Peggy Downing
Segra and Stargull by Peggy Downing